MW00913252

Blossomed

A Minded Story

Blossomed: A Minded Story
Copyright © 2016, Celie Bay Publications, LLC
All rights reserved.

No part of this book shall be reproduced or transmitted in any form or by any mean, electronic, mechanical, magnetic, photographic including photocopying, recording or by any information storage and retrieval system without prior written permission of the publisher. No patent liability is assumed with respect to the use of the information contained herein. Although every precaution has been taken in the preparation of this book, the publisher and author assume no responsibility for errors or omissions. Neither is any liability assumed for damages resulting from the use of the information contained herein.

This work is a work of fiction. Names, characters, places, and incidents either are a product of the author's imagination or are used fictitiously, and any resemblance to actual persons, living or dead, business establishments, events or locales is entirely coincidental.

Published By: Celie Bay Publications, LLC

ISBN: 978-0-9962803-9-6

Edited by: Kelli Collins, Edit Me This
Interior book design by: Bob Houston eBook Formatting
Cover Design: Tonya Ridener, Double J Graphics

Blossomed

A Minded Story

By

R.L. Merrill

Dedication

This story is dedicated to the amazing educators and parents who care for our special needs children. You make the world a better place every day for each and every one of us.

Blossomed

On Samhain, the veil between the spirit world and the material world thins. Anything can happen, including the rebirth of those souls who weren't given the chance to blossom to their full potential. One such soul had accepted her early death as her destiny. Fate has much more in store for her.

The woman sat in the dingy gymnasium and listened with one ear to the tales of woe being shared by the others in her support group. She'd been here for an eternity, or so it seemed. It had been so long, new members rarely noticed her anymore. Some folks would try to talk to her, include her in the group, but she was more than satisfied to hear others speak. They had much more interesting things to talk about.

"Dear, you haven't shared recently. Is there anything you'd like to share?" Grandma asked her.

The woman smiled at the matron whose presence she'd come to find as comfortable as a warm blanket in front of the fire on a cold winter's night.

Comfort was difficult to find for people like her. They suffered from D.D.S., or Death Denial Syndrome. The support group was a place for them to experience an awakening, establish awareness, and ultimately, achieve acceptance of inevitable circumstances. The woman knew she was dead, had been for some time, but she didn't want to move on yet. She hadn't had much life. In death, she found relief from her pain, but the longer she listened to these people talk, the more she yearned to hear more of their experiences. It was as if she could live vicariously through their love stories and adventurous escapades. All the things she'd missed out on.

It took effort for her to speak, words leaving her at an alarming rate the less she used them. She'd forgotten her own name. Even her thoughts were vague and gray around the edges. She'd noticed in the beginning of her time here that some of the others who'd been there even longer had eventually faded away. Some fought their existence and would just blink out. Some were given other choices.

When she finally opened her mouth to speak, she realized she was now alone with Grandma.

"I'm sorry, my dear. I couldn't wait for you to find the words. It has been decided that you will be reborn. Since you haven't made a conscious choice, one has been made for you. The time is near and you will be sent on."

"But...I don't want to go back. I had a life, short as it may have been. The only reason I stayed here so long was—"

"I understand, dear. It has been decided for you. I just wanted to prepare you. You won't have an escort for the first part, so you will be on your own. Someone will meet you to help you…"

She felt a stirring in her body, one that she might have equated to a rapidly beating heart if she could recall what that felt like. Before she could protest any further, the sensation spread rapidly throughout her limbs. She began to pant and felt as though she was starving for oxygen.

"Your rebirth will be over quickly. I wish you strength and courage on your journey. It will give me great pleasure to see you find happiness."

A roaring sound filled her ears as she fought against a wave of pressure. She opened her mouth to scream just as everything went black.

***

Justin frowned as he strummed his guitar. No matter how many times he tried playing the chords, they just didn't sound right. It had been six months since the accident, and while he'd come much further than the doctors told him to expect, his patience with himself was running out.

He flexed his hands and winced at the lingering stiffness and pain. They were better, much better, but they just didn't want to cooperate sometimes.

He looked at the clock and saw it was time for his daily walk. Schedules and structure kept him sane, always had, but more so now that he wasn't quite at full capacity. His cognitive testing showed that some of his function had still not returned. He attended speech therapy five days a week for two hours each time and tried to relearn what had come so natural to him before. Doctors explained that where he was a year after the accident was likely where he would be for the rest of his life. That was not satisfactory for him.

"Blossom! Come. Do this."

Blossom, Justin's four year-old Great Dane, loped over to him, panting happily. She sat obediently while Justin attached her leash, her tail thumping excitedly on the rug. His girl had been a huge part of his recovery. Knowing she needed him to pull through this made it that much more important to him that he get well.

The two hopped in Justin's Range Rover and cruised across town to the San Leandro Marina. Justin was grateful he'd been cleared to drive. He preferred to walk near the water. When they arrived, he helped Blossom down from the SUV, concerned about her "delicate situation," even though his brother Jason told him not to be worried. He still wanted to clobber his brother for allowing his girl to get knocked up. Jason bred Danes with his wife as a hobby. He took care of Blossom while Justin was in the hospital and then in rehab, until he could care for her himself. He'd had a friend's stud over for a weekend to breed with his own Dane, Blossom's sister, and hadn't realized Blossom was in heat.

"It's an omen, dude. You needed a reason to get your ass movin'. I gave you several good ones! Just wait 'til you're a daddy. You're gonna love it!"

Great Dane puppies weren't exactly something Justin had planned on. His life needed to be a well-oiled machine: write, record, tour, repeat. The accident had already thrown everything off course. He just wanted things to get back to normal. He refused to accept that they never would.

It was dusk and a bit chilly as they set off, the sun setting over the Bay in pinks and lavenders. The two walked along the coastline, Justin taking care to keep his pace slow enough for Blossom and for his weary legs. He'd been fortunate to not break any bones in his limbs when he was thrown, but his head had taken a dangerous impact that had the doctors concerned. He still had issues with balance and speech…and sometimes his hands just didn't take orders. He'd been incredibly lucky on all accounts, but for an overachiever like Justin, a creative force of nature, limitations like those he was experiencing were just not something he could sit back and accept.

Speaking of sitting. Blossom had taken a seat and was staring off towards the water. Justin tried to give her a tug, but she wouldn't budge.

"Come. Make mile marker. Come on." He gave one more tug, but the one hundred thirty pound beast sat unmoved. Justin looked around to see if anyone else's dogs were acting weird, but there was no one nearby. She'd stopped about three feet from a bench, so Justin decided to take a load off, thinking maybe she just needed a breather.

"Fine," he huffed, trying to muster up some patience. He stretched his arms and legs out, feeling a bit of relief, and followed Blossom's line of sight.

The water was eerily calm. No waves broke against the rocks below the path, only faint ripples moving across the usually choppy water. Justin took a deep breath, wishing he could pick up the scent of the water, even if it was rank today, just to know that he could. Instead, he settled for the slight breeze against his face that blew his light brown hair out of his eyes.

A melody he remembered from something he was working on before the accident played through his mind and he started to sing, his voice growing in volume as he realized no one was around to hear him. The vibrations in his chest reminded him of the fact that he was alive, against all odds. He sang until he felt tears sting his eyes, letting out his frustrations. His speech might be damaged forever, but he could still sing his heart out.

Blossom lay down next to his bench after a few minutes of his singing, something she often did at home as well, and rested her chin on her front paws. She began whining softly, still staring out into the water. Justin reached down and scratched behind her ears, whispering to her that everything was okay, but her whines grew more insistent.

"Pain, girl?" Justin worried perhaps they were getting too close to her due date for her to be out walking, even though Jason assured him she had time.

"Enough today. Go Uncle Jason."

It took a few tugs to get her attention away from the water. She kept looking back as they walked to the car.

***

The sound of his voice awakened her from her watery rebirth. She could hear it soar tenderly across the surface. When it stopped, she finally opened her eyes.

The saltwater was dark around her and stung her eyes. She blinked hard and then swam toward the faint light above. It felt eerily like her death, but she somehow knew things were different this time. She broke through the water and breathed for the first time in her new body. She saw the figure of a man and his dog walking away from the coast and her eyes followed them as they got into a car and drove away.

The woman was on autopilot. Her body seemed to know to swim to the shore, where she found a sandy area hidden by some bushes. She took a few moments to calm her breathing, shivering from the chilly air against her cold, wet skin. Instead of panicking, which she was pretty sure she would have done in her previous life, she laughed. And laughed. And laughed until her voice went hoarse.

She held out her arms and examined them. Everything looked different. She was meatier, her skin paler. The wet strands of hair that clung to her skin were shades of brown that seemed foreign to her. Her legs were longer and fuller. Of course, the body she remembered had been riddled with cancer. Being ill for months before finally succumbing to the disease had left her body wasted. *This* body was hearty, full of energy.

"If you keep on laughing, the whole world will know a naked, wet, formerly dead woman has just washed up out of the Bay. Get yourself together, woman."

The man's heavily accented voice startled her. She crawled farther into the bushes.

"Oh, for the love of the Old Chap! Dude, you might have a little more tact. Makes the job easier, or hadn't you noticed?" The woman's voice sounded playful, not angry.

The woman peeked out from behind the shrubs and blinked. Standing before her was a guy with a tall Mohawk, dressed like some punk rocker, and a beautiful woman with long locks of curly blonde hair, wearing a black party dress. They were complete opposites. His brooding stare intimidated, her flirtatious smile invited.

"I brought you some clothes," the woman said, approaching her with a small duffle. "There's also a new ID, money, credit cards, and keys to a car parked just over there in the lot," she said, gesturing with her thumb over her shoulder. "I think I finally have Grandma convinced they can't just pop you guys in here with nothing and expect you to not freak out." The blonde winked and crossed her arms over her chest, accentuating her curvy figure.

"Go on and get dressed, then. We have things to explain to you." The man turned away and the woman made a face behind his back.

Who were these people?

"You ever hear the expression 'you catch more flies with sugar?'"

"No. It must be another one of your backwoods Louisiana phrases a proper person wouldn't be caught dead using."

She listened to the man and woman bantering back and forth, her teasing, him sounding annoyed. Once she finished dressing in black stretchy pants, tall black boots, and a long white tunic, she stepped out from behind the bushes.

"But I *am* dead, silly! And I don't care what you say; you have your own quirky British uppity sayings that are just as bad. Come on, Louis. Nobody says 'cock up' with a straight face."

The man, Louis, started with a comeback, and then his lips split into a reluctant smile. "Bloody hell, you do go on. It has nothing to do with... Never mind."

The woman smiled victoriously, then noticed her.

"Wow! You are stunning." The woman circled her and whistled low. "I'm Maggie, by the way." She stuck out her hand and flicked her head in the man's direction. "Don't mind Louis. He's so much fun to mess with. Now. You probably didn't get the whole deal from Grandma, but you were sent back for a reason. You have a task to complete. We all have to do one before we can move on, but in your case... You gotta help this dude. His name is Justin and he's a mess—"

"Margaret," Louis said in a singsong voice. "You're supposed to let her figure it out, darling. Wouldn't want to drop a clanger."

Maggie laughed at him, bending at the waist. "That is precious. You are so adorable when you try to insult me using your antiquated sayings. Come on, Good Charlotte! Let's get you prepped. The year is two thousand fourteen and you're in—"

"Two thousand fourteen? Are you serious?" So much time had passed! The last date she remembered was...

"It's been over thirty years, love. You passed just after I did. The world has changed a lot. People are still imbeciles, though. Bunch of bloody assholes, if you ask me."

"And we didn't. There are still plenty of good people." Maggie frowned at Louis and put her arm around the woman. Charlotte. She liked it. "Look. You will know what to do when the time is right. All the information you need to function in this time is up there in your fancy new brain. For now, let's get you to your car. Are you familiar with this area? You're in San Leandro, California."

Charlotte had to think. She'd driven some around the Bay Area. She'd grown up in Newark, which wasn't too far away. She remembered the Nimitz Freeway ran north to south, so if she could find that...

"Here we are," Maggie said as they approached a large vehicle. It was some sort of Honda, she recognized the symbol on the front, but she'd never seen anything like this.

"It's a big box! What—"

"They certainly have made cars uglier. Damn Americans want everything bigger. Don't they get it? They're killing the bloody planet with these beastly—"

"Alright, Mister Doom and Gloom. Can it!" Maggie may have been telling him what to do, but she was all sass and no bite. He seemed to be irritated with everything *but* her. Charlotte was so entertained by them she almost forgot why she was here.

"Do you have any questions?" Maggie was asking her.

Charlotte had a million, but one stood out.

"So whenever I do what I'm supposed to do, is that it? They'll take me back? Because I—"

"We've no return instructions for you. I'm not certain what that means. It appears the Old Chap Upstairs decided... Bloody hell. You must have something very important to accomplish, or must have made a great sacrifice—"

Charlotte held up a hand for him to stop. She didn't want to think about sacrifice or anything involving her past. What was done was done. "Fine. I guess I'll figure it out. So, um, where do I go? What do I do?"

Louis stepped up next to Maggie and put a hand on her shoulder as she started to speak, effectively silencing her. She looked up at him with an adoring expression and nodded.

"That's as much as we can say." Maggie stepped away from Louis and approached Charlotte one last time. "Here," she said, handing her a pocket watch. "Keep this. If you need us—"

"Margaret—"

"Oh whatever, dude! I got this. Don't I always got this?" He rolled his eyes and looked toward the sky, mumbling under his breath as he walked away. Maggie followed him toward the darkness that was rapidly dropping from the sky.

"You'll be great," Maggie called back to her. "Just remember: listen with your heart. You've come through the veil for a very good reason." Louis tugged at her and she protested. Then he swatted her on her ass. Hard. She yelped and took off chasing him in her heels, yelling all kinds of colorful profanity at him.

Charlotte smiled and then shook her head. As if being born from the water of the Bay wasn't strange enough, her two greeters...

She stood there wondering what the gigantic plastic doohickey attached to the keychain was for, then she noticed the buttons. Somehow it all made sense. She clicked the key fob. Once the door was open, she set the duffle on the driver's seat so she could rifle through its contents. Inside she found a passport, a wallet with a California driver's license... *Oh, for the love of God.*

"Charlotte Bay. Is my name. Really." She laughed and placed the documents back in the bag. She looked down at her clothes and shrugged. Hopefully she wouldn't look as out of place as she felt.

She tossed the duffle into the backseat and slid into the driver's seat, praying silently she remembered how to operate a motor vehicle after her time spent in wherever she'd been. The car appeared to be an automatic, thank goodness, and started right up.

Now if she only knew which direction to head...

***

"We're back here," Jason shouted from the backyard as Justin slammed his door shut. He walked around to the back, shaking his head at the number of cars parked on the Castro Valley street his brother lived on. Jason and his wife Gia had picked up this house when the housing market had taken a dive, with money she'd inherited previously. It was a great house with a huge lot that climbed the side of the hill in terraces.

Justin opened the rear door and let Blossom down easy, straining a little under her weight. The two of them went through the side gate, tripping over some garbage bags left out from a recent party, no doubt. Gia and several of her girlfriends were gathered around a fire pit, holding hands and chanting. He felt the heat from the flames but couldn't smell the smoke, another awesome symptom of his fucked-up situation. Blossom wandered over to where her sister Buffy was sleeping on a twin mattress Jason put out for the two mamas-to-be. Jason raised his beer from his seat on the second-level terrace. Justin climbed the steps and collapsed wearily into the lounge chair next to his brother, watching the women with a little confusion.

"Samhain, dude. Remember? Oh, man. Sorry. Yeah, it's their yearly ritual. They're trying to offer a blessing or sacrifice or some shit to the spirits who cross the veil on this holiday. See, the veil between the spirit world and ours is at its thinnest tonight, so anything can happen, dude."

Justin frowned. "Anything?" Not likely anything he *wanted* to happen. He'd love for the full use of his hands back. To be able to speak normally. Hell, he'd like to be able to smell again, for the headaches to go away…

"Yeah, bro. You could even get laid! Look, you know Shelagh's been after your ass since last year. And there's Deirdre," he gestured with his head. "She's the one who did that love spell last year."

Justin groaned and rubbed the back of his neck. He'd come over to have dinner and had noticed something tasted weird in his wine. Deirdre had stared at him all night, as if she'd been waiting for something to happen. Jason and Gia were so high they just laughed the whole time, until Justin got fed up and left. That was before the accident. Now he figured his lady-killer days were over

"Sorry. Keep harem. All you."

Jason snorted. "Nah. Not since we got married. No more of that fun. I do miss it sometimes. Those witches, man. All kinds of enthusiasm, if you get what I'm saying."

Justin and his brother differed in so many ways, unlike many twins they'd met over the years. While they might look identical, Jason was your typical slacker. He had mean talent on the bass and could sing almost as well as Justin, but he was satisfied with their small-time success, driving a van and towing a trailer to gigs, shit like that. Justin had always been a perfectionist. His O.C.D. didn't allow him to just kick back and let life happen. He *made* shit happen on his own terms. Yet another reason his limitations were frustrating the hell out of him and most likely the cause of his intense migraines.

Blossom climbed up the steps and came to lie at Justin's feet. He bent down to scratch her distended belly. "Make sure okay. Acting weird. Marina. Pain?"

Jason perked up a bit and got serious. He ran his hands over her body. She flopped over onto her back and put her paws up in the classic "pet me" pose. The brothers laughed at her dramatic groans.

"She's not bleeding? Eating okay? Any complaints when she's moving around?"

Justin shook his head. "Nah. Moves slower. That's it. Week, right?"

Jason shrugged. "I think so. Pretty sure she conceived around the time Buffy did. Maybe we should have her looked at by the vet tomorrow if you're worried, but I think she's fine. I'm not getting any bad vibes or anything."

Justin rolled his eyes. "Hocus-pocus."

Jason sat up and looked sternly at his twin. "Don't be disrespectful just because you don't understand, bro. There are forces at work that—"

"Sorry. Wish...more faith. I don't. Now."

Jason frowned. He leaned forward and put his hand on his brother's knee. "I want you better, man. It's going to happen. You just need to relax. Stop pushing so hard."

"Don't know stop," Justin whispered softly, his voice drowned out by the women's laughter. Their circle broke up and they passed bottles of wine around. Someone turned on some music, some of Justin's. He grimaced.

"Have to?"

Jason laughed. "You know what it does to them! Hell, *I'll* probably get laid tonight, thanks to your sexy man voice." He slapped him on the shoulder and asked, "You need a drink? Beer?"

Justin shook his head. "No. Need brain cells." *Fuck, I sound like an idiot. Why won't it come out right?*

Jason laughed, but Justin didn't think it was all that funny. The reality of living the rest of his life damaged like this was settling in hard. He wasn't going to give up or anything. He just had no clue what he would do with himself without his music.

He leaned back in the lounge chair, pushing hard against the arms to get the damn thing to lie back, but he didn't quite have the coordination to make it work. He groaned and shifted once more, causing the chair to lean back quickly, almost flipping him over. He finally got it balanced and rested his head on the attached pillow. He smiled when he saw the stars peeking through the clouds.

A light came on to his left, catching his attention. *Huh.* No one had lived in the cottage next to Jason's place in a long time. The owners had moved away and didn't want to rent it out in case they came back. But someone was there tonight.

Jason came walking up the steps with a beer and a bottle of water in his hand. Justin took it from him and thanked him, then gestured with the bottle at the house next door. "Light next door. Owners back?"

Jason cocked his head to the side. "Uh-uh. Jim would have been over here after beer already. Nah, I got no clue. You think it's a squatter or something? Maybe we should, like, check it out, man."

Justin made a face at his goofball brother. "What, check out? Peek windows? Remember up there? House on hill? Pit bulls shotguns meth lab? No thanks."

Still, he couldn't help but wonder. He'd had a strange feeling all day, like something was brewing. He thought it might be Blossom and the pups. Now he couldn't be sure.

"C'mon, bro. Let's go jam. You'll feel better."

Justin hoped his brother was right. They'd been playing together most nights. Singing came back easy. Why the fuck he couldn't talk, but the lyrics came right back, was beyond him. The doctors explained that he had Broca's Aphasia. His injury had occurred in the left hemisphere of his brain, and since music was a right-brain function, it hadn't been impaired. If his hands would cooperate, playing should come right back. He couldn't do much on guitar, so Jason had been playing his parts. Some nights they had friends fill in on bass and drums, but it bothered him. He hated the others seeing him weak like this, but if he wanted to keep this machine going that was their band, Rivers, he had to accept help. He didn't like it, but it was a fact of his new life.

***

Charlotte decided to just drive, and she ended up somehow at the address on the new driver's license she'd found in the duffle. The house was up high on the hill on the border of Castro Valley and San Leandro. She didn't remember being there before, but her body apparently knew what to do. This was going to take some getting used to.

She pulled the Honda Element into a driveway in front of an adorable cottage. It was perched on the side of the hill, with a long gravel road between her house and the one next door that led up the hill into some trees. She sat for a moment looking at the house, wondering just what she was walking into. She fingered the keychain with the car key on it and assumed the other key was to this house.

She got out slowly and looked around the neighborhood. From her perspective, she could see into the backyard of the home on the other side of the gravel road. Several women were laughing and carrying on around a fire and she heard some dogs barking. There were houses closer together across the street, but on this side, the houses appeared older and spread out.

Taking a deep breath, she thought, *here goes nothing*. She grabbed her duffle and closed the car door, then climbed the steps to the front door of the cottage, which had a large porch and flower boxes hung on either side. She inhaled the aroma from the sweet pea vines and the freesia growing there and smiled. She'd always loved flowers and thought if this was really her new home, she was going to have a blast planting.

The key did indeed open the lock easily on the door. She stepped inside and sniffled a little at the dusty, musty scent that hit her. She closed the door but immediately opened every window in the place. She discovered it was a two-bedroom cottage with a large bathroom containing a claw-foot tub she couldn't wait to test out. The décor was mostly done in white, which was going to make cleaning a bit of a chore, but it all seemed so bright and cozy, she was anxious to make it hers.

She pushed her nagging fears about what she was doing aside and proceeded to start cleaning, finding a fully stocked cabinet under the sink in the adorable kitchen, full of all she'd need.

After a good hour of dusting, pulling down shears and stripping beds for washing, she finally stopped to take a breather. She was more and more amazed by the minute at all of the updated gadgets that she miraculously knew how to use. A digital thermostat to control the temperature, a mop with disposable sheets, a bagless vacuum cleaner, computerized front-loading washing machine and dryer, a microwave, lamps that turn on by touch, ice and water dispensers on the front of the refrigerator... This was just weird. Laundry was going, the place was inhabitable, and there was food in a pantry that hadn't expired, so she was all set.

Suddenly, the sound of loud guitars growled from the house next door, startling Charlotte so badly she spilled the glass of water she'd poured herself all down her front.

"Well, let's hope there are clothes here that will fit me." She stripped out of her pants, which got most of the water, and tossed them in the laundry room to add to the next load.

The guitar was now playing a tune that stopped her in her tracks. The sound was amazing, and it filled her with joy and all kinds of other sensations that had her new body swaying back and forth. Soon she was dancing and laughing all over the house.

When the voice, *that* voice she'd heard at the water's edge, started a husky crooning...

Her heart began to pound and goose bumps broke out over her whole body. Her nipples hardened. This was the sound of ecstasy, of everything sensual and sexual she'd never experienced but always yearned for. Her skin felt so hot she almost tore off the tunic she was still wearing, but realized she still didn't know if she had any other clothes in the house, and every window was still open and bare, the lights from the house probably lighting the entire street.

Charlotte giggled and ran through the house, closing windows and pulling shades and blinds down one by one until all that was left was the bedroom window, which faced the house that glorious sound was coming from. She thought about turning off the lights and spying, but then the music stopped abruptly and she heard male voices shouting.

Charlotte pouted and went back to doing laundry, throwing in the last of the bedding. She peeked into the closet and the dresser drawers, sighing in relief that there were clothes for her. And scrubs? She wondered if she had a job set up for her and everything. She still struggled with the idea that she was moved into some house that had things for her and food…

Nope. Time to move on. She had something she was supposed to do, and Lord knows she'd spent enough time being idle.

She decided to try out the tub while she was waiting for the rest of the bedding to dry so she would be able to go to sleep. She passed a stereo coming out of the bedroom and turned it on, smiling at the tunes coming from speakers all around the room. It was a fancy setup, one she'd thought she wouldn't be able to operate, but somehow her fingers just knew what to do.

The music was similar to what was coming from next door. The name Highly Suspect flashed across the display and the title of the song must have been the other line. She watched the lights on the stereo and got lost in the sound. The next song that played showed the artist was Jack White. None of these names sounded familiar, but then, the last music she remembered hearing that made her smile came from The Tubes and some newcomer from England named Billy Idol.

She stood there listening for one more song before finally walking into the bathroom, pulling off the tunic and tossing it across the room and into a hamper with ease, as if she'd been doing it every day. The water came out hot and the bath salts she found smelled delicious as she added them to the flow. She sank into the water slowly and sighed with happiness. Water had always soothed her. She wondered if it was a coincidence that she'd been born into this body in the water. It had to mean something. She was just too tired to think about it at the moment.

She stayed in the water until it cooled, wrapped herself in a towel and bounced back to the bedroom in time to the music playing. She danced around for a bit longer until she dropped from sheer exhaustion onto the bed. Her eyes fluttered closed and she had almost drifted into sleep—when she heard a noise outside the open window.

***

"*Idiot*," Justin whispered harshly at his clumsy brother. Jason had slid on the gravel and cursed loudly just as Justin was peering over the bushes and into the window.

The woman was wrapped in only a bath towel, with another one around her hair. She was splayed across the bed peacefully, until Jason's ridiculous racket woke her. She sat upright, the towel falling from her head to reveal a mass of wavy brown hair that clung to her pale skin as she looked around, alarmed. Justin barely had time to duck below her line of sight before she discovered him creeping.

He was completely awestruck by her. The blue of her eyes pierced his heart, and she hadn't even looked his way yet. She was everything he'd never known he wanted in one glance. He just couldn't figure out what it was about her that drew him in, captivated him. It was almost as if someone had paid attention to every little detail about a woman he'd ever found attractive his whole life and molded them into one beautiful creature.

Sure, he'd written silly love songs about falling at first sight. Whatever. This was way more than that. He had to know more. He had to—

"Dude, what the fuck are you doing? She's going to call the fucking cops!" Jason at least had the common sense to stay hidden. Justin was struggling to remain crouched. He wanted to touch her face, trace the curve of her bare shoulder...

Then she was standing in front of the window, looking out into the night, probably to see what was making the noise. Justin could see her silhouette from under the bush and watched hungrily as she looked around and then pulled the window down to close it.

"What is *wrong* with you?" Jason stood in front of him with his hands on his shoulders.

Words had completely left Justin. He opened his mouth to speak several times as his brother watched him helplessly.

"It's okay, bro. Just breathe. It's okay. Let's—"

"Can I help you with something?"

The brothers turned to find the object of their snooping perched at the end of the porch, watching them with a humorous expression. Jason put his arm around his mute brother and laughed.

"Sorry, ma'am. We didn't know someone had moved in. I live next door. Name's Jason, and this is my brother Justin."

The woman leaned a hip against the railing and raised an eyebrow. "I just got here tonight."

The headache came on suddenly. Justin pressed the heel of his hand into his eye, praying this one didn't last long. He leaned into his brother, who caught his weight with an "oomph."

"Is everything alright?" she asked again. Her voice made Justin's heart hurt.

"Yeah, he's fine," Jason said nervously, patting his brother on the head. "He's just a mess. Well, welcome to the neighborhood. Let us know if we get too loud." He started to pull Justin away from the house, which made his head pound even harder.

"Oh," the woman exclaimed with a smile. "I was enjoying that. You guys have a good night." She turned to walk back into the house, then looked over her shoulder. "You sure he's okay?"

"Positive," Jason answered, dragging Justin farther away. They'd almost reached the fence when Justin finally got his brain back online.

"She... More."

Jason laughed at him and pulled him inside the gate. "That's a helluva way to meet girls, dude. You can't go peeking in their windows, man. Although, damn. This neighborhood just upped its hotness factor. Did you get a load of—"

Justin turned on his brother and swung, missing Jason's jaw by a fraction of an inch. "Don't. She's..."

"Yeah. I got it. Well, you better get your lips moving next time, then. What happened? I thought you were over those spells? You've been doing so much better."

"What if...not? What if... never right again? Don't want...be idiot brother."

"Don't worry. That's my job," Jason said with a laugh, rubbing his hand over his hair. He wore his longer and shaggier. They'd had to shave one side of Justin's head to do the surgery, so he decided to go ahead and shave off both sides and the back, just leaving the top long with bangs hanging over one eye, unless he put stuff in it so it'd stay back.

For the first time, the two of them weren't being confused for each other, at least visually. Justin had always stood out as the more articulate one. The smarter one. Jason was the guy everyone wanted to party with, the guy who knew how to have a good time, but wasn't expected to be a leader.

Their band had really taken off the past two years. They'd been playing festivals and clubs all over the country most of the year, with breaks in between so Jason and his wife could have time together with their dogs and to try to make babies, which, sadly, they'd been unsuccessful with so far. Justin was always a little jealous when they were off the road. He envied the relationship they had, weird as it was. Gia was a white witch and spent a lot of time with her Wiccan friends doing stuff that Justin tried not to ridicule. It just seemed silly to him, but his brother was beyond happy. He was totally enamored of his wife and the two of them had crazy sex all the time, something else Justin envied.

Someday…if his brain would work.

He was so tired of the complications.

"Hey, you want to play some more?" Jason grabbed another beer and traded heated looks with his wife across the patio. Justin sighed.

"Nah. You. Stuff to do. Get Blossom and —"

He pressed his hand into his eye again and tried to breathe. The pain was really bad tonight. He was going to have to call the doctor. Jason approached and put his hand on his back.

"You aren't going home tonight. Let me get you two set up in the back." Jason had built two small cottages on the hill behind the house for when Gia's friends stayed over or he had puppies to keep contained. He called for Blossom to follow and walked Justin up the hill to the first cottage and got him inside.

Jason told him the bed was freshly made, as one of the girls had stayed over last night.

Justin collapsed onto the bed and groaned. "Sorry. Okay morning."

Jason tucked him into the double bed and then patted the mattress next to him so Blossom would hop up and keep her daddy warm.

"I love you, brother. Peace to you."

Before he slipped into sleep, Justin heard Gia's voice speaking softly to his brother.

"I wish he would just stay here. I'm so worried about him."

"I know," Jason answered, his voice cracking a bit. "He wants his independence, but I'm worried about these headaches. I'm so grateful he has Blossom. She knows what he needs. Let's just hope everything goes okay with her delivery. He can't lose her."

Justin instinctually reached out and laid his arm across Blossom, taking comfort in her warmth. She sighed, made an old lady noise and stretched, wiggling closer to him.

They'd slept like this every night since he'd been released from the rehabilitation center. She was his anchor to this world that frustrated him so.

***

Charlotte had a hard time falling asleep and when she did, she dreamed of that voice. She dreamed of a man drowning in pain who needed a life preserver. She knew she should throw it to him, but swam to him instead. He grabbed on to her in a panic, and the two of them started to sink, but then she found the strength within her to kick and swim to the surface. Her strength held them afloat as he began to breathe normally again.

She sat up with a start and looked at the clock. She had somewhere to be.

Totally on autopilot, she showered and changed into a pair of light blue scrubs with rainbows and clouds on them. She shoved some food in her face and grabbed the ID and money from the duffle bag, shoving them into a purse she'd found. The pocket watch, she slipped into the front of her scrubs, feeling it heat up against her skin through the thin material.

She locked up behind herself and trotted out to the car. Just as she had done the night before, she started the engine and just drove, her new brain directing her as she crossed the town and pulled up in front of a small house next to a gas station. A mural painted on the side of the house showed happy animals playing together. She hurried into the entrance and found herself in front of a counter.

"Welcome, Charlotte. We're so glad you could start today. Let's get you set up with a locker." The woman seemed friendly and obviously knew who she was.

She let her new brain guide her and found herself doing the job she'd trained for in her previous life. Sadly, she'd never had the career she hoped for. Cancer in her teens kept her too sick to attend much school, but she had managed to complete a veterinary technician course through the regional occupational program before becoming too sick to function.

It had taken two more years for the cancer to kill her, two years she'd spent in and out of hospitals before finally wasting away in her bedroom surrounded by her grieving parents and sisters. She'd tried to assure them that she was fine, that she wasn't afraid to die. She'd known her death would be hardest on them and tried her best to make it easy.

The morning went smoothly and she was just about to take a quick break to grab a drink when the door opened and two familiar voices filled the front office.

Charlotte gasped. It was her two peeping toms and a majestic harlequin Great Dane. She watched through a crack in the door as her coworker Lisa helped them.

"What's going on with our girl?" she asked.

The one who had spoken the night before leaned on the counter with his elbows and smiled lazily at Lisa, flicking his hair out of his eyes.

"Our little mama here seems to be more uncomfortable with these pups than we'd anticipated. Just want the doc to look her over and make sure all is well."

The one with the shorter hair kept a hand placed protectively on the dog's back the whole time. She leaned into his leg heavily, causing him to stumble a little and smile down at her.

"We'll get you into a room in just a minute. Charlotte," Lisa called out.

She came through the doorway and met Lisa at the counter.

"Sure. If you'll follow me to room three?"

***

Justin wanted to slug his brother for the "wink, wink, nudge, nudge" he had going on. He still wasn't feeling great after sleeping in a smaller-than-usual bed with Blossom, who'd sprawled across his chest as a way to wake him up this morning, then drooled all over him. Now he was faced with this mysterious woman. Again.

She led them down the short hallway of the makeshift office, which used to be a house, and directed them into the last room. It was a tight fit with the two brothers, Blossom and her current wide-load state, and this amazing woman with a huge mane of curly brown hair. She smiled shyly at Justin.

"Which one of you is Justin Rivers?"

Jason nudged him and he opened his mouth to speak, once again finding it hard to find the words.

"I."

That's it. That's all that came out. Justin stood there staring at the woman. Her big blue eyes were wide with anticipation. He hated to disappoint her. He tried and—

"He is. I'm his brother Jason. He'll be back online soon. So what's the deal with his girl?"

Charlotte was her name, Justin recalled. Her name was now playing on a loop in his head as he stared at her so hard his eyes were burning.

She gave Blossom a pet and asked, "What has you concerned today?"

Justin scratched the back of his neck and pressed his lips together. She smiled patiently. Jason came in again for the save.

"Justin said she was acting kind of funny yesterday afternoon, kinda whining and moving a little slower—"

"Water. At water. Bay. Marina. Charlotte." He winced and looked down at his shoes. How much more awful could this possibly get?

"Good morning, Misters Rivers! How's our girl?" The vet they usually saw, Dr. Morrison, came in smiling. Blossom wagged her tail happily and leaned into the petite woman.

"Whoa, girl. You're big as a house! How many pups are you going to have, I wonder? Charlotte? Can you please bring me my stethoscope? I left it in back."

Charlotte smiled at her before turning her gaze back on Justin as she walked towards the doorway...and ran into the wall.

"Oh! You guys saw that, right? It just jumped out at me?" She laughed, shaking her head as she walked out of the room.

Dr. Morrison and Jason laughed, but Justin was so frustrated, all he could do was clench and unclench his fists. His words leaving him hadn't been this bad since he was first in the rehab center.

"And how are you doing, Mr. Rivers? I'm so glad you're recovering from your accident."

Charlotte walked in as Dr. Morrison was speaking and stopped in her tracks, looking at Justin with worry.

"He's better. Just the words sometimes escape him, you know? But he's doing great. We'll be going back out on tour after the pups are born and ready to be weaned, as long as Justin is ready. He's singing again, but the playing—"

"Jason," Justin was able to finally get out. He hated it when his brother talked about his problems, but it was especially humiliating for this woman to hear about his weakness. He shook his head and pressed his lips together again, trying to keep control of his speech.

Control. What a joke. He had very little these days. The more he tried to hold on tight to everything, the more it slipped away.

He turned to the only presence that eased his troubled mind. Blossom. He knelt down beside her and held her face in his hands, letting her lick his ear.

"Alright, Blossom. Let's go get your weight and check on a few things. We'll be back. Charlotte?"

***

Charlotte had thought she had everything under control, until he walked in. That voice. She'd walked into a wall! It all went downhill from there.

Once they'd taken the dog into the lab, Charlotte struggled to help the doctor take her rectal temp, which thankfully hadn't dropped yet or there'd be pups on the near horizon for him, and he didn't seem quite ready for that. The dog ended up knocking her on her ass and then proceeded to lick her face in big, slobbery strokes. She loved this dog instantly, but was quite mortified.

"You've been Blossomed," Dr. Morrison had said with a laugh. "Happens when she likes you. She's a little exuberant."

"I'll say."

Then after they left, she spilled a urine sample they'd fought to get from a cat, knocked over a cart and sent sterilized utensils flying everywhere...and the kicker? She slipped on the cleaner she had just used to mop and her new body sprawled wildly.

Her back hurt and her hamstring was seriously strained by the time she left her first day of work. Dr. Morrison gave her shoulder a squeeze on the way out.

"You're a trooper, Charlotte! I'm glad to have you on board. I'll see you Monday."

At least she still had a job. It was scary to think her mistakes may have cost her the only stability she had in this new life.

She drove home and took a moment to collect herself before climbing out of her car. The house next door was full of life and activity. The women were once again in the backyard singing and laughing around the fire. Charlotte froze for a moment and let their voices wash over her. Their song was in another language, but to Charlotte it was a soothing balm.

Music had always been a source of comfort for Charlotte in her brief previous life. She'd spent hours sitting next to her stereo in her room, playing 8-tracks and records, and then cassettes, in between listening to the new FM radio stations that were playing some really cool rock music. It was an exciting time. Disco was so popular for so long, and then finally new musicians were coming out, mixing pop music and punk sounds from Britain. Music had been her companion during the long hours she'd spent in bed, too sick to move.

She shook off those morbid thoughts. She knew she had been sent here for a purpose and she intended to do whatever it was. Then she'd go about figuring out how to live in this new world, where people carried around phones in their pockets and could find information about anyone or anything with just the flick of a finger across a tiny screen. Her new brain recognized everything and guided her to understand what to do. That didn't mean she wasn't tired from the effort it took to keep putting one foot in front of the other and pretend she wasn't freaking out on the inside.

A wave of exhaustion hit her as she stumbled toward the steps. She sat down hard at the top and put her head in her hands, trying to muster up the energy to get inside, shower, and —

"Ma'am? Alright?"

In the fading light, she looked up to see the man with the amazing voice approaching her slowly. He had his dog with him and she was pulling on her leash to get close to Charlotte. She finally tugged so hard the leash came right out of his hands and she bounded up the walkway to attack Charlotte with big wet kisses.

"Oh…Blossom, no! Come… Come…"

It was no use. The dog turned her head to glance at her owner, but was entirely too busy licking Charlotte to follow his directions.

Charlotte threw her arms around the dog and laughed, scratching her around the ears and hugging her close. "It's fine. I could use this hug right now."

The man—Justin was his name, she remembered—stopped a few feet away and slid his hands into his back pocket.

"Sorry. Never does this."

"Really, it's fine. She must know I needed a hug."

He cocked his head. "You're new. Here. Vet. I never before." He was doing that thing again where he pressed his lips together. Charlotte immediately remembered what Dr. Morrison had said about his injury. No wonder he'd had such a hard time talking to her.

"Today was my first day," she answered hesitantly. "I haven't worked in a long time." *That's an understatement*, she thought.

"Oh. I. Sorry…last night. My brother—"

"No, it's okay. It's nice you were watching out for your neighbor. Makes me feel a little safer." Now why did she go ahead and say that?

One corner of his mouth turned up, almost forming a smile. It was the first time she'd seen him without a scowl of concentration. He was so much more handsome when he relaxed his features.

"Moaned. Hurt? You fell sort of." He stepped a little closer and Charlotte remembered how he'd found her.

"Oh, I'm not…I fell earlier. At work, after you left, I slipped. Yeah. Everything's just starting to hurt. I'll be better after I take a bath and drink some tea." *And crawl into bed*, she thought. But that made her cheeks hot. How much had he seen the night before? She couldn't believe she'd been parading around in a towel with the window open.

Justin stepped closer and held out his hand. "Here. Help." He cursed under his breath and then pressed his lips together again, but he left his hand outstretched.

Charlotte placed her hand in his and looked up into his concerned face. She allowed him to pull her to his feet, which put them face-to-face, as they were close to the same height. His eyes were wide as they studied her. His light brown hair fell over one eye, but the sides were shaved close. She could make out the scar on the side of his head. He noticed her looking.

"I. Motorcycle. I'm—"

"Does it hurt?" Before she could stop herself, she reached up to touch his scar. He dropped his head a little and a small sound of frustration escaped.

"Not when...touch me," he whispered. He looked up suddenly and must have realized how close they were standing. "I'm. Get you inside."

***

Justin stepped back and picked up Charlotte's purse, then grabbed her elbow to help lead her up the stairs. He cursed his stupid brain silently, not wanting to call any more attention to his issues. He turned to call for Blossom, but she was already on the other side of Charlotte, pawing the door to get inside.

"Sorry," he muttered, and the vivacious woman just laughed.

"She's a demanding girl, I'll say!"

She struggled a little with the lock before the door opened. Justin's feet felt as if they were in cement. What was he supposed to do in this situation? Follow her inside?

"I do have a favor to ask," Charlotte said, turning to face him. "Oh. Come in. Please. I was going to ask… The teakettle is on the top shelf. As much as I've been a klutz today, I don't need to add another fall to my list of embarrassments and smack my head— Oh! God. I'm sorry."

"Don't be," he said, feeling a foreign muscle working in his face. He was actually smiling.

Her face lit up with a smile of her own and her blush began to fade a bit.

"That looks good on you," she murmured, then the blush was back. "I'm sorry. I just haven't talked to anyone in a really long time."

"I. Talking. Hard sometimes." *Like now.* He wanted to kick himself repeatedly. That was one thing he hadn't tried to get his brain functioning again. He was willing to do anything at this point to be whole, especially in her presence.

"Like the words aren't there when you need them. They just leave you and you're sitting there with your jaws flapping…"

How did she know? She seemed surprised at her words as well. Awkwardly, she pointed at the cabinet and then winced, her hand coming to her lower back.

"Man, I really messed something up. Can you?"

Justin opened the cabinet and reached up easily for the kettle, but then his fingers didn't want to close over the handle and he almost dropped it. He managed to get it to the counter safely and turned toward the sink to fill it with water.

"Thank you," Charlotte said quietly. "I'm just going to go shower. Quickly. Did you want to make some tea?" She seemed shy, as though she wasn't sure about having him there, though not afraid.

"Tea?" He meant where was it, but his question made it sound like—

"Yeah. You know, something herbal? There're some tins over the stove. I'll be right back."

She hurried from the room and he heard her giggle as Blossom followed her. He listened as he set the kettle on the stove and turned it on. Charlotte kept up a conversation with his dog as if she was talking to her best girlfriend. They carried on as long as it took the water to boil. The kettle whistled and still he stood there, listening to her voice. She had such a nice voice. It made him think of honey, like the honey he should be looking for to go in the tea.

Tea. Right. He opened a cabinet and pulled down two mugs. They had puppies on them.

He heard the shower running. He swallowed hard. That meant she was going to be naked.

Justin hadn't always been great with women. Scratch that. He hadn't always been great with women *after* having sex with them. The during was fine. He could hold his own. It was just afterwards, even if he liked them, he kinda didn't know what to do. Feelings and shit. Not his area of expertise.

His songs were mainly about the things in life that frustrated him. Even before his accident he was kind of a frustrated person. Things were never good enough. *He* was never good enough. He spent way too much time being disappointed. Now that he had reasons to be grateful, namely that he was alive and had his whole life ahead of him, he didn't know how to let go of that angst.

"Are you okay? Are you having another headache?"

How long had he been sitting there?

Charlotte stepped over and turned off the kettle. She was wrapped in a long burgundy robe that hung loosely on her body, as if it belonged to someone else. She smiled at him sitting at the table as she set tea bags in each of the mugs and then poured in the hot water. She paused for a moment with her hands on her hips, looking at the cabinets.

Justin watched her movements carefully, thinking they looked familiar.

"Forgot where put something?"

Charlotte turned on him with a worried look.

"I just. I forget. It happens. How you're standing."

She laughed and turned her back on him again. She looked back and forth between two cabinets before opening the narrower one of the two.

"Bingo! Great. Can't have tea without honey."

When she turned back around, she looked nervous. She set down the mugs on the table and held out the bottle. "Did you want some?"

Justin frowned and took the bottle from her. He knew the movements, but his hand wouldn't listen to his order to squeeze. He passed it between hands for a moment and only two of his four fingers would close, so he added his other hand, but he only managed to press his palm against it. Somehow it was enough pressure to get a small stream of honey out. He realized she'd stood next to him the whole time and hadn't—

"You look like you got it," she said, shrugging her shoulders.

She hadn't taken the bottle from him and said something like "here, let me."

Gia was always trying to rescue him out of these tight spots and it drove him crazy. It was a big part of the reason he refused to live with them, opting instead to try to go it alone in the San Leandro house he and his brother had grown up in. His parents had long since moved to the desert, citing the warm, dry weather as a balm for their aging joints. They were enjoying their retirement immensely and were pleased that the boys had chosen to keep the family home, tiny as it was.

When Gia's grandmother passed away and left her a load of cash, she and Jason bought their home two blocks over from Justin's place. It meant the twins were still geographically close, but in their lives, they were miles apart. Sure, they had their music and were making it, slowly but surely, in the indie rock scene. Until the accident...

"I. Go," Justin said softly. He started to stand, but Charlotte put a hand on his shoulder.

"Can I try something?" She stepped behind him and placed her hands on the sides of neck. Her hands were warm and they relaxed him. He sighed and leaned back against the chair. She worked the stiff muscles in his neck and managed to break through the tightness at the base of his skull, taking care not to use too much pressure.

"I used to get headaches a lot. My mother used to do this to make them go away. Is it helping?"

Justin was so far gone he just moaned, which made her giggle. She kept up the expert massage until his neck felt so loose he was afraid he wouldn't be able to hold his own head up.

"Your hands. Amazing." He reached up to take one in his hand and turned it to look at her palm. She had ordinary hands, very pale with medium-length fingers. Her nails were short and unpainted. The lines in her palm were different. Instead of a long life line that wrapped around the bottom of her hand. It branched off in the middle of her palm, faded, then began again. It wasn't dark like the rest of her lines. It was faint.

"What is it?" she asked.

He didn't answer, just ran his finger down the center of the palm observing the way her veins were so close to the surface of her wrist. He turned her hand over and looked at the back. She had light freckles but no scars. Her skin was soft, like you'd expect a newborn's to feel. There were no cracks or callouses. Just pale, beautiful skin.

He brought the back of her hand up to his cheek and rubbed it against his face, feeling her warmth.

"Um...Justin?" Her words broke the spell he'd been under and he let go of her hand quickly, feeling like an idiot. He stood quickly and turned to face her.

"Sorry. I'll—"

"I was only going to say your tea is getting cold. You don't have to go if you don't want to." She looked a little sad and Justin wished he could take back everything.

"No. I don't... Know anything," he said with a humorless laugh. "My accident. Six months ago. Keep waking...think 'today better.' Then forget. Can't tie shoes. Leave water...running. Come back...still on. I'm lost. Glad alive...just don't know...how..."

***

Charlotte understood more than Justin would ever realize. She'd only been alive for a day, twenty-four hours, and it was exhausting. Her new brain ran things for the most part, but it took conscious effort to not speak of things she shouldn't.

Like right now. She wanted to tell Justin everything, thinking he'd probably relate to what she'd been through. During her treatments in her past life, there were times she thought that sure, it was great to be alive and all that, but it sucked a lot of the time, too. She'd known she should feel grateful, but it was so hard...

"I don't always know how to do it, either. I think when you tell yourself you've got all the answers, you only set yourself up for disappointment."

His eyes shot to her with more clarity than before. She knew she couldn't tell him everything, but whatever she'd just said reached a part of him that needed to be touched.

He moved toward her quickly and before she could protest, he wrapped her in his arms and laid a kiss on her, full of all kinds of frustration, anguish...and passion.

It was a foreign emotion. She was startled. He must have realized and pulled back. But it only took a split second for her to catch up to him.

Her hands grabbed his face and she kissed him back hard, knocking teeth with him. Instead of being upset about it, he kind of growled. He increased the pressure of his hold and moaned against her lips. He pressed his whole body against her and she stumbled back into the cabinets.

He spoke an apology against her lips and she laughed. He pulled back, looking as surprised as she felt at how they were acting. She didn't want to stop. This was one experience she'd waited a lifetime for. She somehow knew it was part of her purpose here.

"Whose robe? This?" he spoke against her throat as he kissed her greedily, his full lips doing amazing things to her skin that would probably leave evidence behind.

"I don't know," she answered honestly. "I just found it." It sounded stupid, but he didn't seem to care.

"Don't want. Touch. Belong someone else," he said, breathing heavily. He leaned his head against hers and whispered in her ear. "Tell me. Out of line. Stop."

"Don't stop. I'm just me. It's just me. No one else touches me," she said clumsily. *What the hell kind of answer was that?* "Don't stop, Justin. Please."

That smile was back. And it was hungry. Her words seemed to spur him on. He pressed her up against the counter, his hands gripping her hips hard.

"Up," he said as he sucked on her bottom lip.

The pulls from his lips combined with the gentle swipes of his tongue had her body on fire. Her head fell back, pulling her lip from between his teeth, and he made a frustrated sound. He pushed at her like he was trying to get her up on the counter, so she hopped up using his shoulders for leverage and opened her legs a bit to accommodate him. He stood there staring at her and she thought maybe she'd misunderstood him. She clutched at the front of her robe, eliciting a groan from him.

"No. Beautiful. You. Please."

She loved his choppy way of speaking. He seemed to care less about it in this state. Feeling brave, she untied the belt of the robe and reached for him. He flicked his fingers anxiously at his sides. It was as if her womanhood had blossomed in this new body, making her desirable to this man who wanted her. Wanted to touch her. So why wasn't he?

A growl sounded behind him, causing him to turn. Blossom was in the doorway staring at them.

"Go. Down, girl," Justin ordered, but she lifted her head and woofed at him.

"Maybe she needs out?" Charlotte said with a giggle. Justin looked from her to the dog and frowned.

"Come back?" he asked with a worried expression.

Charlotte hopped off the counter and moved right up into his space. She kissed him on the neck and said, "Hurry. Take care of her. Then let me take care of you." She smiled as she walked out of the room, grabbing her tea on her way out.

***

Justin hurried back to his brother's house, letting himself in the back gate. Blossom went up to the top section of the yard to do her business. Gia's friends were sitting around drinking beer and wine and a few of their male friends had joined them. He found his brother in the kitchen with Gia in almost the same position he'd just been in next door. The thought made his skin feel tight all over.

"Hey, where'd you come from?" Gia asked him, pulling away from Jason, who protested loudly. "Have you eaten yet?"

"No. Need him."

Gia giggled at him and looked to Jason, who seemed confused but followed as Justin grabbed his shirt and dragged him toward the back of the house.

"What is going on with you, bro? You look like—"

"Need something. Like condoms. Courage. *Jesus*." He rubbed at the back of his neck, his palms all sweaty from nerves.

"You mean that chick? From the vet? Next door? No Way! She's hot, dude. Here," he said, reaching into his bedside table. "I don't know if I have any that aren't expired. Shit," he said, bringing out a box with one inside. He shook it into his palm and looked at it.

"Nope. Expired last summer. Fuck. Wait a minute." He pushed past Justin and went out back. "Hey Simon," he yelled. "Dude, come here for a sec."

Simon was a friend and a fellow musician. He'd been jamming with them for a while and there was talk of having him play drums for them on their next tour, if Justin could even play. He wasn't going to think about it tonight.

Simon joined them in the hall and gave Justin a bro hug. "What's up?"

"Dude, you got any condoms?" Jason had no shame. *Dammit.*

Simon laughed, surprised. "Uh, not on me, why? I thought you guys were trying to get knocked up?"

"Not for me, asshole. For my bro here."

They both looked at Justin, who was ready to run for it. His heart was pounding so hard he thought they could hear it over the loud music from out back.

"I. Shit." What would he tell them? That somehow this woman showed up out of nowhere and had his already messed-up head a mess? That he thought feeling her skin against his would be the perfect balm to his fucked-up life? Fuck it. That he wanted to lose himself inside her beauty for a night and see if he was truly still alive and not a shell of a man?

"Don't say a word. Come on." Simon grabbed Justin by the arm and dragged him out of the house. Simon's truck was parked close to Charlotte's driveway and he made a beeline for it, pulling a stumbling Justin behind him. He opened his back door and pulled out a backpack. He dug around in it for a minute before shouting in triumph.

"Yes! Here. There's six. That's all I got, dude, but you're welcome to them."

Justin started to protest, but Simon shoved them at him and closed the door.

Jason ran up and pulled the three of them into a huddle.

"Alright. You remember how to do this?"

Justin slugged him in the gut.

"Alright, alright. When you get ready, you let her lead, man. Don't get all up in your head and—"

"Dude! He ain't a virgin! It's just like riding a bike— Oh, fuck. That's probably—"

"Never mind," Justin said, shoving the condoms into his back pocket and frowning over the bulge they made there. "Jesus. Like kid. Fucked up. Now. Jason?"

His brother put his hands on his shoulders and stared him in the eye. "You are the least fucked-up person I know and you need this. You need to quit worrying about everything and just enjoy yourself. She's a beautiful woman, bro. Is she on board? I mean—"

"Yeah. Um. We…"

"Right. Okay. You get in there and you, well, you get *in there*, you got it? We'll be out here pullin' for you. I mean, not really, but in the metaphorical sense—"

"Got it. I… Thanks. Sorry. Pain in ass. I. Just thanks, bro."

They hugged and communicated as only twins could. Justin knew Jason only wanted the best for him, and he held no anger or irritation toward him. He'd been nothing but supportive since the accident and Justin knew instinctively he always would be. It was a comforting thought in this whole insane life of his. He always had his brother.

Blossom came trotting out from the backyard and leaned into Justin's side.

"I guess you're taking her with you," Jason laughed, putting his arm around Simon. "Did you save any of those for yourself? Cuz I think Deirdre—"

"Fuck that, dude," he said as the two of them walked away from Justin. "I heard what she did to your brother. I'm good. I might just watch those two blondes. They've been all over each other and that Matt guy. They might even have started. Shit, let's go!"

Justin chuckled as the two dumbasses ran back towards the gate and slammed it behind them, a chorus of cheers erupting when they returned.

He looked up the driveway to Charlotte's house. The light was on at the back, where her bedroom was. He thought he might panic. *What the hell am I doing?*

The front door opened and there she was, her silhouette informing him she was still wearing the robe. All may not have been lost. He walked up the drive towards her, telling himself that running in and tackling her on the floor was probably not the most romantic way to seduce her, but it took all of his willpower to stop himself from doing just that.

Blossom bounded up the walk ahead of him and pushed past Charlotte into the house. She laughed at the dog's antics and then turned just as he reached the bottom step.

"She had to do her business?" she asked, leaning against the doorjamb.

"Yeah. She. Yeah." Damn, he was tired of sounding like an idiot.

"I made a bed for her on the floor so she'd be comfortable. I hope that's okay?"

God I'm in love, he thought to himself. He stood in front of her, trying not to breathe hard like he'd just run a marathon. He hadn't even exerted himself. Not yet.

"Charlotte," he said, his voice cracking. He was becoming desperate.

She smiled and held out her hand. "Let me take care of you," she whispered, and pulled him into the house.

He was pretty sure he closed the front door behind him, but he was rapidly approaching a point where he didn't even care. Blossom went straight to the pallet of blankets Charlotte had put on the floor in the wide hallway outside her room and began digging around until she settled down with one of her old lady noises.

Charlotte walked him into her bedroom and turned to face him. She'd lit some candles in two corners of the room and pulled the drapes, he noted with a smirk.

"Is this still okay? I don't want to assume anything, Justin. I'm just glad you're here."

Her words touched him. She didn't treat him with kid gloves, didn't treat him like less of man. She was more like someone who worked with wounded animals and knew how to approach them without making them feel threatened, or in his case, making them feel broken. He reached for her hand and pulled it up to his face, rubbing her flawless skin against his cheek once more, enjoying the sensations immensely. He wanted more of that flawless skin.

"Want. Untie this," he said against her ear, his hands fumbling with the knot she'd redone on the belt of her robe. "I liked. Want."

She reached between them and helped him get the knot loosened. It dropped away, but the pieces of material clung to her breasts, keeping her covered. Justin was dying to uncover her, but the teasing was so exciting. He let his fingers linger over the opening, tracing the seam with both hands, feeling her shiver.

She took in a deep breath and the material split open farther, revealing a strip of pale skin. Justin whimpered. He could barely contain himself. He wanted all of her, but he wanted this moment to drag on, worried he couldn't handle what was in front of him.

That thought gave him pause. He'd never cared for very much foreplay. That seemed really childish to him now. Why had he never savored moments like this? Even when he'd had girlfriends before, their sex had been hurried. He'd rushed. He wanted what he wanted, and then he wanted gone.

But not tonight. He understood a bit more what his brother said about how it was different when it meant something. Tonight meant something.

His touch grew hesitant. He started to shake. He wanted to speak, but didn't trust himself. He clamped his lips together to fight whatever might escape...

"May I?" Charlotte slid her hand under his sweatshirt and gently ran her fingers up his stomach to his chest. It felt so good.

"So good," she whispered, stepping forward to kiss his neck again. Her light strokes against his skin were driving him mad. The shakes were getting worse. "May I?" she asked again.

She began to lift the hem of his sweatshirt and he almost lost it. If he didn't get her underneath him...

Slow. Down.

She pulled his shirt off over his head and smiled at his bared chest. Thankfully he'd been wearing a heavy coat when he'd had the accident. His legs got some road rash. Once he hit the pothole, he was airborne for what seemed like forever before landing on his head, sliding on the asphalt, and then splashing into the water.

He remembered how peaceful the water was. There was no pain, not until he woke up in the hospital after two weeks in a medically induced coma.

Enough of the past, Justin. He needed a whole lot of the present. With her.

Charlotte seemed fascinated with his body. She ran her hands down his chest, over his stomach, until they reached his waistband. She lingered there, as though she was unsure how to proceed, and then she seemed to chicken out. She ran her hands around his waist and stepped closer to him, allowing him access to her neck.

He kissed her there over and over, feeling her response grow more impassioned. She let her hands slide down and she cupped his ass—

Crinkle.

"What is this?"

Oh. Shit. The condoms.

Justin reached behind him and pulled out the noisy wad of wrappers. "Um. The guys."

Charlotte burst out laughing and took them from his hand. "Wow. It looks like we have a lot of work to do if you plan to use all of these." She covered her mouth with her hand, smothering what seemed like nervous giggling. She stepped over to the nightstand and put down the condoms. Justin watched her back heave, as if she was taking in a deep breath. She stood like that for a moment.

"I've never been so excited and scared," she said quietly.

Justin frowned. He knew nothing about this woman. Maybe this was not...

Blossom let out a loud whine from the hallway.

Charlotte and Justin didn't hesitate as they both rushed to her. They found her digging frantically in the blankets as she whimpered and made a low howling noise.

"Is time, girl?" Justin put his hands on her as she lay down, panting heavily. Her huge belly was shifting around and he watched as it tightened up. He turned to ask Charlotte what to do, but she was grabbing towels from the closet.

"Hopefully Blossom'll know what to do, but if she needs help, we'll be there for her." She knelt down next to Justin and touched his shoulder.

***

"I think these pups are coming tonight."

Charlotte was worried for Justin. He looked so nervous. She'd already been able to tell how important this dog was to him. She wanted to be with him, but didn't want to intrude if he had plans to deliver the pups with his brother.

"Done this. Before? Puppies?"

Charlotte smiled. *Boy, had she.* "My parents had Goldens. We had several litters when I was young. Whelping is exciting."

Justin stood up and paced in the small hallway, clenching his fists at his side. "Jason. Should be here. Don't know…"

"Would you like me to go get him? Or I can stay with her? This will likely take several hours. I'm fine if you want to do this here, but I understand if you—"

"She. Whelping box! Comfortable." His speech got choppier the more agitated he got.

"Is the box at your brother's? Shall we take her next door?"

He knelt back down and stroked Blossom's ears. She leaned her head into his hand and let out a sigh, seeming a bit calmer now. "Can move her?"

"Sure," Charlotte said. "Now would be a good time. It doesn't look like her water's broken yet. Do you want me to come with you? Or—"

Justin grabbed her hand hard, hard enough for her to yelp.

"Sorry. Can't. Please. Charlotte."

They were able to get Blossom up and walking with a little effort. Charlotte brought the extra towels with her. Just in case. She'd thrown on a pair of scrubs, not sure how messy things were going to get. She was a little nervous about going to his brother's house with him, but she knew her skills might be needed. Plus, the birth of the puppies was something she did not want to miss. The dog moved a little slowly and stopped to pee twice on the short walk. Charlotte had brought a flashlight and kept a close eye to make sure she didn't drop a puppy on the way over.

Justin led them through the gate to the backyard, where the group of friends was still having a good time around the fire pit.

"Back so soo— Oh! Everything okay?" Gia asked.

"Charlotte. Time."

She couldn't help but giggle at his pronouncement, and Gia looked at him as if she were trying to decipher the Nazi's code. He started to get agitated again, but Charlotte took his hand.

"I think Blossom is in labor. Justin said you have a whelping box set up?"

Gia stood for a moment longer before her eyes grew wide. "Oh! OH! JASON!" she shrieked. "Get out here!"

Two men emerged from a sort of patio room with beers in hand. Through the doorway, Charlotte could see instruments set up. She recognized Jason, Justin's twin, as he approached them.

"Hot damn! Gonna have us a whelping party!" He walked over to Justin and smacked him on the back. "Let's go, Daddy!"

Blossom whined again and leaned against Justin's leg. Still holding Charlotte's hand, Justin led the way up a set of stairs set into the hillside. Their yard went up and up, ending in a line of trees near the top of the hill. Two small buildings sat at the second level, and a third looked as if it were being built on the next level, beside a rather healthy-looking garden. Lights were strung all over the yard, making it easy to see their way up the steps in the dark.

Justin turned towards the cottage on the left and opened the door. Inside there was a double bed, a dresser, a guitar leaning against a chair, and the whelping box. A small bathroom was located at the rear.

"Come on, girl," Jason said, making sure Blossom could step over the short wall of the box. She immediately started digging in the newspaper that had been set all along the bottom. "She'll be comfortable in here. Gia?" he shouted out the door. "Will you bring the towels—"

"I brought some, too," Charlotte offered. She set them down on the bed and stepped out of the way as Gia came in with an armload of towels and a large bowl of water.

"Way ahead of you. This is so exciting! I thought for sure Buffy would go first, but then I thought we had at least three more days. Man, Blossom must have gotten knocked up first, like when that stud first arrived."

Jason and Justin crouched next to the box in an identical pose. Charlotte had so many wonderings about what it was like to be a twin. Her own sister Rose had been only eleven months younger than she and they had grown up incredibly close.

"Is hurt? She?" Justin looked so worried. Charlotte wanted to step in and ease his concerns, but she didn't know how he would feel if she intruded.

As if he read her mind, Justin turned to her and held out his hand.

Shyly, she stepped to his side and took his hand, which he grabbed onto like a life preserver. He smiled apologetically, but didn't let go or let up the pressure. Charlotte thought again about her dream. This all felt orchestrated...

"Just relax, bro. She knows what to do. She's going to be a good mama, aren't you Blossom?" Jason moved around the area like an expert. He explained that he and Gia had whelped four previous litters; their first gave them Buffy and Blossom, then two more litters from that same bitch, and Buffy had been bred once before. Gia had grown up with show dogs and had always wanted to show Danes.

Charlotte wanted to share her experiences and love of dogs, but she knew she should be careful. Dog show folks ran in a tight-knit circle in this area. Chances were she'd met Gia's parents when she was young, or that their parents might have known each other...

She suddenly realized how cautious she was going to have to be about revealing too much of her past life. Would she ever be able to share her secret?

Blossom sat up and began licking herself persistently—and then a grayish blob became visible. Gia and Jason chattered excitedly while Justin just held Charlotte's hand, his lips pressed firmly together.

"Bro, did you want to help with the first one?"

Justin looked to Jason and shook his head.

"Don't. Hurt." He scowled and rubbed at the back of his neck with his free hand. Charlotte squeezed his hand and offered him a reassuring smile.

"It's okay. Sometimes you have to help clean them off and rub them down. It gets them breathing on their own, sort of like a kick-start." He looked at her so attentively when she spoke, as though he were trying to figure out a puzzle. Then he looked back to Blossom, almost as if he were in school and got caught not paying attention to the teacher.

The first pup came out and Blossom got to work licking and cleaning the pup. Jason and Gia cheered quietly, smiles lighting up the room. Being in the presence of new life was one of the most amazing things a person could ever witness. Charlotte was elated to be a part of this experience.

The second pup came and the third right on its heels. Jason and Gia reached in to help clean them off and presented them to Blossom, who licked them persistently before turning to lick herself.

"They're coming fast," Charlotte said. "She's doing great."

Justin moved to Blossom's head and stroked her ears and she lay panting, the first three pups nursing happily on her distended teats.

"Do you know how many pups? Did Dr. Morrison tell you?"

Jason shook his head. "We had her x-rayed, but it was really hard to tell. It could be at least ten. That's how many were in their litter. Buffy had twelve in her last litter. Danes are prone to having a lot of pups."

If that many were coming, they were going to be there a while.

An hour later, the fourth and fifth pups were born and Blossom took great care with them. Gia and Jason cut the cords, explaining that although she was doing a really good job, moms sometimes inadvertently damaged the pups when chewing the cords.

After three hours, there were six pups and Blossom needed a break. Jason and Gia stayed with the pups, continuing to clean them up, while Justin and Charlotte took her outside to pee and drink some water. She still had a good amount of energy. Justin stayed close to Charlotte, grabbing for her hand whenever possible.

"Glad...here. With me. Easier. Scared."

Charlotte beamed at him, feeling completely euphoric. Even if for some reason her time here ended up limited, she could not have asked for a more perfect life. It hadn't felt real, not until she'd touched *him*. He was her anchor to this new life that in many ways scared the shit out of her. He probably felt the same about his life after the accident.

"Do you work, Justin? I mean, can you? After the accident?"

He let go of her and moved a little closer to Blossom, who leaned into his leg heavily. He smiled at her.

"Work?" He laughed. "Not job. Band. Rivers. Me and Jason. Music." He watched her closely, as if he were gauging her response.

"That is work! Why wouldn't it be? Are you guys signed? Are you really big or something? I'm... Wow. I haven't listened to music in a long time." *Stupid!* What if he was like super popular?

He laughed. "Signed, yes. Indie label. This." He held up his hand and put his thumb and forefinger about three inches apart.

"So sort of big? How big? Like really big?"

Justin rested his hands on his hips and looked down at his feet. His shoulders were shaking. *Oh God.*

"I'm sorry! That was an awful thing to ask."

He held out a hand and looked up. He was laughing. Really hard.

"No. Just. Twelve-year-old." He pointed his thumb at himself as he spoke and it dawned on Charlotte what she'd been asking. She covered her face with her hands and felt her cheeks burn.

"Hey," he said up close. He gently pried her hands from her face and held them to his chest. "Show you. Later."

Her eyebrows rose in disbelief. Justin made a face of mock shock.

"Band. Grammy. What else?"

She loved his good-natured teasing. He pulled her to him and she buried her face against his shoulder, sighing happily.

"I hope you show me. Lots of things. Later."

He smiled. "Want." He kissed her gently. Sweetly. Then Blossom leaned into her and she fell against him.

"I guess it's time for more," Charlotte said with a giggle. Justin pushed her hair back over her shoulder and kissed her once more before reaching down to pet his girl.

Blossom led them back to the cottage and immediately climbed into her box and maneuvered carefully around her pups. She began licking herself again just as another pup presented itself.

Five more hours later, there were eleven pups. Justin was fighting to stay awake by Blossom's side. Jason urged him to lie down and rest, but he was determined to stay with his girl. Gia went into the house then came back up the steps, hollering for Jason.

"Buffy's at it now, too! Holy shit! Come help me!"

Jason looked apologetically at Charlotte, but she shook her head.

"You go ahead. I've got this."

Jason ran out to join his wife in the house, leaving Charlotte and Justin alone. Justin's back was to the wall next to the whelping box, and Blossom had been resting her head close so he could rub her ears and calm her. She was exhausted.

"Think. Done?"

Charlotte wasn't sure. There were so many balls of fur all over Blossom's belly looking for sustenance, it was hard to tell what was happening.

Just then Blossom yelped a little and started panting hard. A grayish sac came out and Charlotte was there to grab the pup. She started rubbing furiously with the towel, but it didn't make a squeak.

She cut the cord and then offered the pup to Blossom, who licked weakly at it before laying her head back down. The pup still wasn't breathing, so Charlotte carefully stood up with the pup and spread her legs a bit. She wrapped the pup in the towel and made sure she had a good hold, then with both hands, she swung it down between her legs and back up.

"What?! Fuck! Charlotte—"

The puppy let out a whine then and Charlotte breathed a sigh of relief. "Sometimes that helps get them breathing. I'm sorry."

Justin sat back and relaxed, his eyes drooping, barely awake. "No. Thank you. Beautiful." And with that, he was out.

Charlotte giggled at his little snore and the way his lips hung open a bit. She went to the bathroom and washed her hands, then grabbed a blanket from the bed to throw around his shoulders.

"You did so good, Mama. Are you done?" she asked Blossom.

The dog heaved a big sigh and sat up, careful of her pups. She started licking again, and sure enough, out came number thirteen.

"Holy... I can't believe it!" She helped Blossom with the pup and then sat down, feeling the exhaustion herself. The puppies were all eating, wobbling around, or sleeping soundly. Charlotte looked them over and saw that they all appeared to be healthy and doing fine. In the morning, well, after the sun came up, she'd see if there was a scale so she could get some weights, and maybe even some ribbon to tie on the pups in different colors. There were six boys and seven girls. Charlotte wondered what they were going to do with this many puppies.

Jason came in then, smiling. "Blossom is a much better mama so far. We've had to do most of the work for Buffy, spoiled brat! Everything okay in here?"

Charlotte nodded, looking to her sleeping charges. "I think so. I'm hoping she's done. She's really tired." A yawn escaped her and she laughed. "It's been a really long time since I've done this. I forgot how much it takes out of you."

Jason frowned. "I'm sorry we couldn't be of more help. If you can hang on another hour or so, the sun will be up and I can call one of Gia's friends—"

"It's fine. I think she's done. I really do. It's been probably an hour since the last one came. A baker's dozen, can you believe it?"

Jason's eyes bugged out. "Thirteen? Well! Let's hope that's a lucky number for us. I know Justin wants to donate a few puppies to be service dogs. Seeing how many we're about to have, I think it's a great idea. Blossom has been really good for him."

"Did she actually go through training?" Charlotte asked, intrigued.

Jason shook his head. "Gia has a friend who trains therapy dogs. She worked with her a little, but when Justin got out of the rehab facility, it was like she already knew how to take care of him. He stayed with us for a couple of weeks, but he wanted to be home. They're doing alright, I suppose. I just hate for him to stay alone. Those headaches... The doctors said we still need to worry about seizures...and why am I telling you all of this?" He laughed and rubbed the back of his neck like Justin was prone to do.

"Because I'm here. Because you're worried about him. Don't worry. I know you don't know me very well, but it seems like maybe this all happened for a reason. Me moving here, meeting you both. I'll help however I can with the pups, but I don't want to be in the way or—"

"No! That's not what I meant. No, I'm glad you're here. I know for a fact there's a reason this all happened. I'm just not sure about *him*. He would be pissed if he knew I was telling you anything. My brother is a painstakingly private person. This whole experience has been a huge invasion for him. But he's a lucky son of a bitch. We're all lucky he's with us and in such good shape. His speech will get better. Or it won't. We'll deal with it however."

Charlotte was taking a chance, but she thought if Justin trusted her even a teeny bit, he would rather she heard this from Jason than having to explain it himself.

"Can I ask what happened? Just so I know? I don't want to say or do the wrong thing, you know? I made a crack earlier about falling and hitting my head—"

Jason held up a hand and laughed. "You don't need to worry about that. He mostly has a sense of humor about it. Mostly. He's really frustrated about his speech, but he got to a place where he could tolerate some jokes. Honestly, I don't know how he's alive.

"We had all gone out for a ride into Sunol, not too far from here. Justin didn't ride a whole lot, but he was a very good driver. Very safe. He worried some about the traffic, especially after a friend of ours got clipped on the freeway and broke his leg. His bike was toast, but he was better in no time and bought a new bike. It rattled Justin a little, but he'd still go with us. It was a huge triumph to get him to cut loose and buy that bike like he'd always wanted. If you hadn't noticed, my brother is a little, ah, well... You maybe haven't known him long enough. Anyway. Jesus."

Jason was a funny guy, but Charlotte could tell he was avoiding talking about the accident. Could have been a plethora of reasons why he wouldn't want to talk about it.

"We'd planned to head back in the late afternoon, but we got to talking and it was getting dark by the time we left. I was ahead of him in the canyon, which as you probably know, is pretty dangerous any time of day."

Charlotte vaguely remembered. "You mean Niles Canyon?"

Jason nodded. "Yeah. We planned to meet up at the Florence for a beer with some friends and then drive home together, but when I got there, no one had seen him. He'd dropped back on the road and no one remembered seeing him come out of the canyon. We got some friends who had trucks and went looking for him, called CHP and shit. We found him in the fucking creek, man. He'd somehow gone off the road at a place close to the water, his bike hit a pothole and he and the bike went flying. He hit his head on something before landing in the water. Damn near drowned. The only way we found him at night was the headlight from his bike was shining towards the road. It was awful. Worst night of my life."

Jason rubbed at his eyes and took a deep breath. "We're close because we're twins, but he's more to me than that. He's my best friend. He's my world. I love my wife, and I know we would have gone on if he didn't make it, but the two weeks he spent in the coma were the scariest... I don't know what would have happened, man. I don't care if he never speaks another complete sentence again. I'm just fucking glad he's here."

"Fucking glad," Justin slurred. "Fucking loud. Need bathroom."

Charlotte and Jason jumped at his voice and laughed at being caught. Jason hurried to his side and helped him to his feet. Justin smiled sleepily at Charlotte as they passed her to go to the bathroom.

Charlotte stood and stretched her back, which was thankfully feeling better after taking some Motrin at the house. She heard the brothers knocking around in the bathroom and laughed at their banter. She eyed the bed longingly and wished she could collapse there. Then she remembered the state of her scrubs. *Ew.*

"I'm going to have Gia call her trainer friend, and another friend to come help us out so you two can get some rest. It's going to be a rough couple of weeks, bro," he said to Justin as they came back out of the bathroom. "You need to fucking sleep."

"Will. Not leave Blossom."

"You can stay here, man. But you need to sleep. Let me take you home for a few hours so you can really rest because—"

"No. Here. Not—"

"Justin?"

***

His head was pounding, his whole body ached, but her voice was like a balm against all of his pain. He turned to look at this amazing woman who'd waltzed into his life, what—a day ago? And he never wanted to be away from her. He wanted to know her, wanted to be with her… Was grateful she'd come to him during this dark time. He stared at her as the lightening sky grew brighter through the window, illuminating her from behind and setting her curls on fire.

"So beautiful. Charlotte." He couldn't help what came out of his mouth around her. Didn't care.

"Justin? Do you want to come rest for a bit? At my house? You'll be close. You'll—"

"Yeah, bro. We'll take care of your girl. You go rest so you can be there for her for the next few weeks. The doctors told you—"

"I know. Fine." He let his brother support him, leaning heavily against Jason's side. "Her," he said, looking to Charlotte.

"Come on," Jason said, putting his arm around his brother's back, supporting his weight. "Let's get you to bed. I'll even sing to you."

"Help," Justin said over his shoulder to Charlotte as they walked out the door together. The three of them laughed on the walk over as Jason proceeded to serenade his brother and Justin groaned. "Death. Murder. Torture."

Jason got Justin into Charlotte's house and helped him to her room.

"No. Gross. Shower." Jason laughed and redirected him to the bathroom.

"Alright, I'll get you in, but I ain't washing your ass—"

"I'll take care of him," Charlotte said quietly behind them. The brothers turned to her, surprised. Charlotte shrugged and smiled. "Just get him in the tub."

Charlotte went back to her room and closed the door.

Justin looked at his brother, who gave him a sly smile.

"She'll take care of you. Damn. Maybe I should crash my bike. I could use a sponge bath." He laughed, and then realized what he'd said.

"No," Justin said, shaking his head. "Don't. Okay. Lucky." Justin smiled broadly at his brother.

"Well, then. I guess you have this all figured out. I'll leave you to your slice of heaven then." Jason kissed his brother on the cheek and patted him on the back. He turned for the door when Justin spoke.

"Thank you, Jason. Thank you for everything."

Jason turned to him, startled at the complete sentence. "You… Never mind. I love you."

"Love you, too."

Jason gave him one last teary glance before leaving him in the bathroom.

He stood for a moment, smiling to himself. He had grandpups. He had a wonderfully supportive family who had put up with his grouchy, moody ass for six months. And now? He had a beautiful woman in the next room who wanted to take care of him.

Take care of him. Shit. That meant naked. He was still thinner than he wanted to be. His muscles had atrophied while he was in the coma and he'd lost a ton of weight. At six feet tall, he'd once been two hundred pounds. Now he hovered around one seventy-five, and that was after he'd gained some weight. Would she feel sorry for him? Would his hands stop working when he went to touch her?

He could worry about it, but he'd end up with a headache. He chose to take her at her word, that she wanted to take care of him. He began undressing just as she knocked at the door.

"Justin? Do you want me to run the water?"

"Um. No. Fine. Minute."

"Okay," she called out softly. "I'll check on you in a few minutes."

Justin smiled as he leaned over to start the water. It took a moment for the temperature to go from freezing to scalding, then back to just right. He finished undressing and slowly stepped into the tub, praying he didn't lose his balance. The tub was a huge claw-foot number and the water felt amazing. He lowered himself slowly until he was fully reclined with his head resting on the ledge. A huge sigh slipped from his parted lips just as the door opened.

"Justin, are..." Her words trailed off as she entered.

His back was to her, but he turned and smiled to find her in just her bra and panties. Her hair hung down, obscuring his view of her breasts. His jaw fell open and he could not for the life of him think of a word to say.

"I was going to... Do you..." She was so shy. Her cheeks flushed such a gorgeous color. Justin sat up a little more and turned his torso towards her, holding out his hand.

"Want." The only word that came to mind. He uttered the one word that summed up his entire existence. He wanted. His mind back, his music career, peace... But now Charlotte embodied his want. He wanted her more than any of those other things. Somehow he knew being with her would change his life. Or maybe it was the exhaustion.

Charlotte smiled and said, "Turn back around and sit up for just a moment." Justin did as she asked, waiting impatiently. He felt her hand on his shoulder. "Mind if I join you?"

He made some lame noises, an attempt at speaking that failed. Charlotte carefully stepped into the tub behind him, and once she was settled, she gently pulled his shoulders back until he was resting snugly against her. He slid his hands along her legs that cradled his body. She felt like heaven. As if she were made just for him. For the first time since his accident, he felt comfortable. He wasn't worried about forgetting something, or something on his body not working. He could just *be*. And he intended to do that for as long as she'd let him.

Charlotte reached for a washcloth and soap and gently washed his hands, arms, chest and torso. She lingered at his shoulders and neck, turning his body to liquid peace. He'd been tired when he came in here. Now he refused to give in to sleep. Instead, his body was alive from her touch. He sat up and spoke over his shoulder.

"Let. Me."

Charlotte pulled her legs in and turned her back to him, switching positions. The glimpses he'd had of her beautiful body were so precious. She still covered herself, but he intended to ease her so she wouldn't fear him, or this. This intimacy.

He took the washcloth from her and mimicked how she'd washed him. But then his hands found her breasts, and he lost focus. Their heavy weight filled his hands as his fingers slid over them. The combination of the water and the feel of her smooth skin stirred sensations he hadn't counted on ever having again. Charlotte felt so good. Would she taste as sweet?

"Charlotte. Want."

"Then have, Justin. I want you, too."

Later, when he tried to remember exactly how the best sex of his life had come about, Justin would be frustrated with the lack of detail his brain could recall. His hands, though... They would not fail him. His hands would provide a physical memory for him that would last a lifetime. His lips and tongue would relish the sweet taste of her for years to come. His eyes would recall just how lovely every inch of her flesh appeared as she became his.

Charlotte climbed out of the tub first and handed him a towel. But it was too late for the civility of drying off. He was on her like a shopper on Black Friday was all over the deals at Nordstrom. He touched, squeezed, and took whatever he could get his hands on as he backed her into the bedroom. They fell on the bed, her giggling at his determination.

"Laughing. Why?"

"Because," Charlotte said, placing her hands on his face. "You're touching me like I'm going to go away at any minute. You can relax. I'm not going anywhere. I'm all yours, Justin."

He smiled and chuckled at her words. She was right. He was so overwhelmed by the feel of her that he couldn't decide what to do first. Until her legs fell open. Then he knew exactly what he wanted.

Charlotte responded to his touch enthusiastically. She cried out, she thrashed about, challenging Justin to fight her movements in order to bring her what she so desperately needed. He knew she was close when her movements slowed to match the rhythm he'd set. She shuddered with her passion, her peak causing them both to cry out.

Justin had never loved this act so much as he did when hearing what his touch did to his lover. His Charlotte.

"Sweet. Charlotte."

He didn't give her time to come down before he reached for the condoms they'd left on the table the night before. He tried to roll one on in order to join in her ecstasy, but his hands no longer wanted to cooperate. He groaned as he ripped the first one.

"Hey," Charlotte purred, placing her hands on his. "Let me?"

Her face was flushed such a lovely shade of pink, his cognitive functioning departed him. Her eyes held his as she took the next package from him and used her nimble fingers to open it. She struggled a bit with how to roll it on. "Like this?" she finally asked as she placed it against the tip.

Justin's words were gone, however, once her hand grasped him. She paid close attention to her task, thankfully, and didn't see just how close he was to losing all control. When her fingers got to the base, she looked up with a smile.

"There! That looks right. Did I... Justin?"

All he could do was nod once before he bent to kiss her. In one movement, he pushed her back and fell into the cradle of her legs. He kissed her so deeply she had to pull back for air. He took that opportunity to thrust inside her welcoming body, still quivering with aftershocks.

She gasped and her eyes went wide.

"Justin!"

Their eyes locked and Justin experienced something he'd never had with a woman before—a connection so deep, he felt as though he was making love for the first time.

She wrapped her legs and arms around him so tightly he could barely breathe. He dug his toes and knees into the bed to gain purchase as he continued to drive into her as deeply as he could, encouraged by her moans in his ear. Her body slid up the bed with each stroke until he ran her into the headboard.

"Sorry. Good. Charlotte. So," he spoke as he tried to catch his breath.

Charlotte patted his shoulder just before pushing him over and straddling him. Once he was buried inside her, she took over the movement for them both until Justin wanted to scream. She felt so good, and all he could do was hold on for dear life as she ground against him. She looked exquisite from every angle and Justin appreciated the access he had to touch her everywhere. He knew he was done for when she placed her hands on his chest and dug her nails into his flesh. She threw her head back and began keening as her body tightened even more around him.

"Charlotte," he shouted. Her eyes locked with his as he came in a rush so hard, his body jackknifed off of the bed and he wrapped his arms around her, crushing her to his chest.

"Charlotte," he whispered against her hair over and over, the sound of her name filling his heart with joy. "Good. Charlotte. Love. Charlotte."

***

Charlotte knew she shouldn't giggle at his pronouncement. She felt giddy all over. Sex was way more than she'd thought it would be. Justin was way more than she'd thought he would be.

And love? He'd said love. She felt love for this man who was basically a stranger, and that didn't seem strange at all. They curled up together after their amazing lovemaking and Justin fell fast asleep, his hold on her like a death grip still, even in his unconscious state. But Charlotte's mind was spinning.

She had so many questions. Did this mean she got to stay? What if they came back for her? It seemed unfair that she would meet this man and feel so deeply for him, only to be pulled away from him after...

She glanced at the bedside table where she'd left the pocket watch the woman, Maggie, had given her. She wished she'd receive some guidance—

"Pssst," she heard from the hallway. Maggie stuck her head in the doorway, wiggled her eyebrows, and motioned for her to come out.

That was easier said than done. Justin was holding her so tight, she had no idea how she'd get out of his grasp.

"I got this," Maggie whispered, now at the foot of the bed. She yanked on the blanket covering them until it fell to Justin's waist. He grunted in his sleep and let go of Charlotte with his left hand to grab for it.

That gave her an escape route. Except his hand was tangled in her hair. She crawled away but kept her head next to him. She was still stuck. She used a piece of hair to tickle his nose, causing him to twitch and then yank his arm way from her to scratch his face.

Charlotte swallowed the yelp over having several strands of her hair yanked out and reached for the robe she'd left on the floor earlier. She hurried into the hallway, giving one last glance at Justin, his perfect back now bared to her. He really was beautiful—

"Hurry! I don't have much time. You can go back to ogling his ass in a minute!"

The women giggled together and Charlotte couldn't help but grab Maggie into a big hug.

"I can't believe this has happened! But Maggie, will I—"

"We still don't have any return instructions, which either means you aren't done yet, or it means you get to stay. I think it would be cruel to both of you to pull you away right now. I mean, seriously. That boy is so in love with you, and look at you! You're all glowing and shit! How was it? He was your first, right?"

Charlotte nodded and sighed dreamily. "It was a little crazy at first. He was a little crazy. I'm sure it wasn't his first time, but man…"

She giggled and wrapped the robe a little tighter around herself. She wanted to get back to him, but she had to know.

"Maggie, I want to stay. I can't believe what an amazing life this is! He's so wonderful, and Blossom! The puppies are so amazing. I have a job, a place to live..." Charlotte trailed off, hearing herself talk. Maybe it was too good to be real. She'd better accept that now, otherwise she would be crushed.

"I'm so grateful for this, for all of it. I understand, though. If I have to leave, at least I was given this experience." She barked out a laugh rather than sob with defeat. "At least I won't be a virgin forever."

Maggie put her hands on her waist and popped out a hip. "No fucking way am I letting them take you back. You deserve this happy. Louis showed me what happened to you. He can do that, you know. It was so fucking unfair! I don't care what I have to do, but I'm making sure they let you stay."

"Maggie, love, you don't know what you're saying." Louis appeared behind Maggie with a frightened expression. "You can't make promises like that. You just don't—"

"What? What're they going to do? Send me back to Group? Fry me in the underworld?"

"Something like that, yeah. Bollocks, love. You can't go around making promises you can't keep. They may decide they want something from you in return that you can't deliver. I d-d-d-on't w-w-ant—"

Maggie put a hand to his cheek. "Don't worry. I got this. Don't I always got this?" She winked at him and looked back to Charlotte. "You just go on loving your man. Take care of him. Let this love blossom. But remember, y'all may not be out of the woods yet."

Maggie approached Charlotte and hugged her tightly, whispering in her ear. "Love that man. He needs you. You need him. Love each other, that's all it takes, babe." She kissed her on the cheek then turned to Louis, who looked completely distraught.

She took his hand and said something so low, Charlotte couldn't hear her. He closed his eyes, wincing in pain, and then they disappeared.

The whole exchange shook Charlotte. Now she wasn't just worried about what would happen to her and her newfound happiness, but what if Maggie risked her own happiness in the afterlife because she'd made Charlotte a promise she couldn't keep?

Moaning from her bedroom had her running back to Justin's side. He pressed the heel of his palm into his left eye and thrashed on the bed.

"Shhhh," she said, crawling back in next to him. "Justin, I'm here. Are you okay?"

"Hurts. Blossom. Hurts." He tried to sit up, but the pain hit him so hard he winced, then fell back on the bed with a gasp. "Hurts," he said once more.

"Should I go get Jason?" Charlotte worried for her lover. How could she ease him? "Do you have medicine?"

"No. Drugs. Messed up. Just. Charlotte."

She could do nothing but curl around him and pray.

Several hours later, Charlotte woke to an ethereal sound. She figured she'd been taken back and she was hearing an angels' chorus welcome her to heaven. The light was so bright when she opened her eyes, she thought she'd been blinded. She rolled over and was confused by the aches in her body. If she was in heaven, would she still feel as if she were run over by a truck?

A truly heavenly sight greeted her as her eyes came into focus.

Justin entered the bedroom with a plate and glass of juice. Singing. She recognized the old Doors tune. He was wearing a pair of low-slung jeans that hugged him right below the hipbones and no shirt. He must have had Jason bring him clothes, because they'd both been covered in puppy afterbirth when they came here. The smile on his face had her sure she was dreaming.

"Awake. Hi. Breakfast." He set the items down awkwardly on the bedside table, slyly grabbing for the used condom wrappers and tossing them into the trash, his cheeks red.

Charlotte stretched her arms up over her head. "This must be heaven. That smells delicious."

"Not. Close." He leaned down to kiss her and she melted into the mattress at his touch. It felt so good. But then she remembered her conversation with Maggie. She wanted to cry at the injustice.

"Can't," he said with a frown, pointing at the food, then at his nose. He shook his head. "No smell."

"You can't smell? Oh, man. Well, that explains how you can kiss me this morning," she said, covering her mouth with a giggle. For however long she had, she must put on a brave face.

As much as she yearned for a life with him, the important thing was that *he* have a life, the life he was meant to have.

"Not," he shook his head, frowning. "Not bad. Good. Sweet. Charlotte." He bent down to kiss her again, but this time he stretched his body over hers, kissing her insistently. It was as if since he couldn't express how he felt verbally, he intended to impress his feelings upon her physically. Impress. Hmmmmm.

"Want. Can't. Blossom. Need check on."

"Of course. I'm sorry I slept so long." Charlotte pulled the sheets up to cover her chest, self-conscious now that it was the next morning. What if she'd prematurely assumed that there was any permanence between them? Would he say goodbye now that they'd made love and that be it? *Oh God.* She'd been thinking all kinds of things, but she knew from her past life that men didn't always stick around after using the L-word.

"I can help if you like, or… If you need to go, I understand. I don't want to assume anything."

"Please!" he exclaimed, grabbing both of her hands, squeezing harder than he probably meant to. "Want. Charlotte. Please. Be with me." He jerked back and pressed his lips together. "I want…be…with me."

The smile that lit up his face was completely triumphant. "Charlotte!" he cried, bouncing a little with excitement. "Be with me! With me! Love…" He blinked and swallowed hard. "I love…Charlotte."

His smile was more tentative now. Charlotte sat up and pressed her hand to his cheek. Her heart was bursting. Tears filled her eyes but she made herself smile. She would give him whatever he needed. He'd already given her more happiness than she'd had—

"I'm so happy, Justin. Let me clean up and I'll help you."

He didn't let go of her hands. "Not just help. Be with me." He was so serious. Charlotte felt as though he were telling her something of real importance.

"Okay. For as long as you want," she said, swallowing a huge lump. Could she keep that promise?

He leaned in to kiss her, tenderly this time. He pulled back and touched her wild hair with a smile.

"Eat," he urged. "Then Blossom."

"Right," she said, reaching for the plate. He'd scrambled some eggs and made toast. She scooped the eggs onto a fork and hid the fact that she'd just crunched on some shell. She smiled at him and nodded.

"Thank you for breakfast." She ate a few more bites and then washed them down with orange juice to remove the traces of eggshell from her mouth. He was very sweet to cook for her.

"More?"

"No, thank you. This was perfect. Just give me a minute."

She kissed him on the cheek. As she crawled past him to go to the bathroom, she swore she heard him say, "Want."

She showered quickly and braided her hair to keep it out of her way. She went back into her room. He was attempting to make the bed. She bit her lip at the sight of his narrow hips as he bent over to tuck in the sheets.

"I'll just be a minute," she said, grabbing a bra and panties from the top drawer of the dresser. She found some jeans on a shelf next to a few sweatshirts. Another shelf on the side had a stack of t-shirts She shrugged and figured she'd go with that and grabbed a sweatshirt in case she needed it. She hurried past him and went back into the bathroom to dress.

She'd never been naked in front of anyone other than her mom, sister, and doctors before. He'd seemed to really like her body. Hell, she did too. She just wasn't sure she could get used to being naked with someone so easily. Now, she thoroughly enjoyed seeing *him* naked. He was thin, no doubt from his accident, but she loved the way he looked, loved the way he felt even more. He had barely any body hair; just a light dusting over his chest and down his abs. The hair on his legs had felt so soft as she'd run her hands and feet over him. And the things he did with his hands and mouth...

And he said he loved her. Was this crazy? It felt crazy.

She threw on the clothes and smiled again at her reflection. She had the kind of face now that didn't really require makeup. Her big blue eyes were so dramatic and she loved the color of her eyebrows and eyelashes. She brushed her teeth, laughing at his comment about not being able to smell her breath, then paused. He'd had so much stolen from him.

She vowed to not take anything from him without making sure he knew just how much it meant to her.

They closed up her house together and held hands as they walked next door. They found a zoo around Buffy. All of Gia's friends were over, gawking at the little black, white, and gray pups.

"My brother! Congratulate me, dude! I'm a father of ten!" Jason hugged his brother, who was smiling like a loon.

"Ten. Thirteen. Twenty-three!" Justin shook his head. "Lot of poop."

Jason's smile changed subtly. "Yeah, man. You look good, bro. You get some rest?"

Justin squeezed Charlotte's hand as he smiled at her lovingly. "Feel good. Charlotte."

"Yeah, I bet. Listen, your girl is doing great. Carina stayed with her today and she said she's happy to come over whenever you need a break for a few hours. Gotta make sure you rest, bro."

Justin nodded. "Thank. Her. Go." He tugged on Charlotte's hand and she smiled at Jason over her shoulder as they climbed the six or seven steps leading up to the second level to Blossom's little cottage.

"Hey, Justin," Carina said as she stood. She looked surprised to see Charlotte behind him and stifled a giggle. "Your girl looks great. She's been up a bit. Still pretty tired. These pups are taking a lot out of her but she's a good mom."

Justin nodded but went straight for Blossom's side. Charlotte smiled and held out her hand. "Charlotte. Thanks for watching them."

Carina shook her hand, her eyes wide. "Carina. Jason said you're a new vet tech at Boulevard Pet Hospital. That's where I take my dogs. How do you like it?"

Charlotte pushed a stray lock of hair back from her face nervously. She'd gotten by without having to answer too many questions. She hoped that continued.

"Great, so far. Yesterday was my first day. I go back Monday." Thankfully she had tomorrow off, too, so she could give Justin a hand. She worried he hadn't gotten enough sleep—

"They have a good staff there. Where did you work before?"

"Oh, I haven't worked for a while. I was…um…gone. For a while. I just got back."

Justin looked at her and smiled curiously, but then Blossom started licking his face.

"Gone. Huh. Okay. Well, good luck! I'll come back tomorrow so you guys can have a break. Take care, Justin." She smiled and waved, giving Blossom a scratch on the head before leaving. Charlotte tried not to freak out. What would she do when they all started asking questions about her? She could tell this woman was more than just curious. Her questions felt almost interrogative, as if she felt protective over Justin.

Gia and some other girls popped in to visit and chatted briefly with Justin. He mostly just smiled and nodded. Charlotte noticed he really didn't talk much around others. Had he always been like that?

When they were alone, he stood from the floor and stretched, then he took Charlotte's hand and tugged her over to the bed, sitting down and patting the bed next to him. He took a deep breath and pressed his lips together in deep concentration, as if he had something really important to say. Charlotte tried not to panic.

"Know don't know," he said, gesturing from himself to her. "But meant. Can't explain." He rolled his eyes and bounced the heel of his palm off his forehead, like "of course I can't explain because I can't talk." Charlotte smiled and waited for him to finish.

"Have questions. Don't care. Just want. Charlotte." He took her hands in his and inhaled a big breath. "Not whole. Not stupid. Still sing," he said. She could tell how hard he was struggling, but didn't want to interrupt him.

"Don't know happen. But want this. Charlotte. Can?"

"Are you asking me if we can happen?" she asked, her heart pounding. He nodded with a hesitant smile.

"Yes. I want to see what happens, too."

"You gone. You here? Staying?"

Oh God.

"I don't know. I want to. It might not be up to me." How else did she explain it?

He frowned deeply, unhappy with her answer. "Leaving?"

Charlotte shook her head. "I have no plans to leave, no. I want to stay. This is all new to me," she said, wondering if he'd get her meaning.

He was quiet for several moments before he tried to speak again. "New too. Want stay. Have therapy. Days. Hours. Play night… Rehearse. Tour again. Hard."

Justin turned away from her and rested his elbows on his knees, looking down at Blossom. His eyes followed the movements of all the bundles of fur.

"Staying," he chuckled. "Two months? Puppies?"

"Oh! Yes. Puppies will be able to go to new homes in two months. Ish. If all goes well. Jason said you were going to donate some for service dogs?"

He nodded. "Want help. Blossom help. Want others." He pressed his lips together and winced a little. "Need Blossom. Hard."

"I understand. I can't believe how much you've accomplished on your own."

That was apparently not the right thing to say.

"Care self. Fine." He slapped a hand against his chest as if to say he was fine on his own. Charlotte blew out a breath and shook her head.

"I'm sorry. I just know how hard it is to be sick and have to depend on others. I know it had to have been hard for you. You're so independent."

"You? Sick?"

Uh-oh. *Shit.*

She shrugged. How the hell was she going to get out of this one? "I just know. It was a long time ago. I'm fine now. Look, I can't—"

"Charlotte," he said, taking her hand again. "Okay. Can say ready. Just want you. Now. Past over." He rolled his eyes. "Getting over."

She smiled at him. He had come a so far and was probably going to struggle with his speech for a long time. Maybe forever. But strangely, she didn't need to hear his words to figure out what he needed, or wanted to say. She felt as though she understood him on a deeper level. It was probably more frustrating for him than anything.

"Are you hungry? Can I get you some food? Then we can stay with Blossom until you're tired. I'm guessing you'll be sleeping here with her? Do you need anything from your place?"

"A lot."

Charlotte blushed. She had asked several questions. "I'm sorry."

Justin held up his hand. "No. Fine. Food yes. Sleep?"

"Yeah. I just meant, I thought—"

"You sleep. Me. Us. Want."

Her blush burned through her cheeks the more he spoke.

"I'll stay as long as you need me," she murmured, looking away.

His frown said he didn't like that answer, but he seemed to be getting tired with the strain of this conversation.

"Let me go get us some food and see when they fed Blossom last. Okay? I'll be right back."

He smiled up at her as she stood from the bed, and he watched her walk out the door. As she went down the steps, she turned to see him at the window looking out at her. She waved and he waved back, his smile like a lovesick puppy. She was sure hers looked exactly the same.

She ran into Jason first as she entered the house.

"Hey! How're things?"

She took a deep breath and glanced around. Several of the women were watching them and she really needed to speak to Jason alone.

"Can we?" she asked, gesturing with her head toward the kitchen.

Gia looked up and caught what was going on.

"Yeah, I made a lasagna. Why don't you come and get some for you and Justin?"

Charlotte nodded and followed Jason into the kitchen, where they were finally alone.

"How's my brother? I mean, how was he? Did he sleep?"

"He did. We did. Today. Not sure how long. Maybe a few hours? He needs more, for sure. Listen, Jason—"

"I could tell by the look on his face that something monumental is happening. I'm all for it. I also know that you have no idea what you're getting into with him, and that kind of sucks. I hope you don't spook easy."

Charlotte shook her head with a frown. "Not at all. And I know that he's got a lot of health concerns. I just…I don't know how much of what he's said to me… Jason? Is he pretty clear? I mean after the accident? I know his speech—"

"He's totally in his right mind. He's just as stubborn, willful, brilliant, and frustrating as he always was. He knows what he wants and accepts nothing less. You can trust that whatever he says, he means. Why? Did he say something?"

"He says he wants to be with me. I just didn't know—"

Jason's face broke into a huge goofy grin. "Far out. That's awesome! Do you feel the same?"

"I do. I...really care about him. He's wonderful. I just..."

"Look, he's got Aphasia. His speech is fucked up. He gets headaches, his hands don't work the way he wants always, and he can't smell anything. Other than that, he's like any other man out there walking around. With needs and wants. Shit. I don't mean to be crude. I'm happy to see him happy. He seems happy with you. I hope you two can just let this flow, you know? See what happens."

If he only knew, Charlotte thought to herself.

***

Four Weeks Later

"Justin!"

He couldn't help it. When she put on those scrubs in the morning, she looked so damn edible. He couldn't keep his hands off of her.

"Want," he said, running his fingers under the elastic waistband of her pants.

She squealed and pulled away, putting her couch between them.

"Want. You are a bad influence! I want, too. But I gotta get to work, babe. I'll be home early today. We're closing at two. I want to help Gia with the Thanksgiving feast preparations for tomorrow."

Charlotte had slid as easily into his family, his life, as an old pair of comfy jeans. They'd established a pretty great routine. Charlotte worked during the week at the vet's office, and he went to speech and physical therapy. Evenings were filled with puppy love and band rehearsals. He'd finally accepted that his playing days were limited. His voice was as strong as ever and so he'd acquiesced to Jason's pleas that they add a new guitar player and make Simon a permanent member of the band on drums. They'd auditioned local guitarists and found a guy they'd met through mutual friends. He also slid into the band like old comfy jeans.

Justin and Charlotte had slept in the room with Blossom and the puppies for the first couple of weeks, but were now very comfortable in her place. He was sleeping better than he had since the accident, and the sex...

Charlotte was completely open and excited about trying new things. She'd finally admitted that she hadn't had a lot of experience before him and was thoroughly enjoying their intimacy. Justin was sporting perpetual wood around her. Every time she moved, it just did something to him. He felt guilty for manhandling her so much, but she'd just giggle and welcome him happily into her body.

Everything was perfect. It was like nothing he'd ever hoped for and everything he never knew he wanted. He was even writing songs again, with Jason's help on the guitar. They were sappy love songs. Mostly. There were a few naughty ones as well that made Charlotte blush whenever he sang them to her.

Jason was ecstatic about this new development in Justin's life. He told Justin over and over how great it was to see him in love. The house was overflowing with sappy shit, what with the four lovebirds, their amazing mama dogs, and twenty three Great Dane puppies, who were getting quite daring with their explorations. They'd finally had to move Blossom and her pups into the patio room with Buffy and hers, to avoid any spills down the stairs or off the edge of the terrace. In the afternoons, under the watchful eyes of all the adults, the pups would wander the first level of the yard and play happily. They'd had to get all kinds of different ribbons to be able to tell them apart.

Justin, Charlotte, Gia and Jason met with the service dog people a few days before Thanksgiving and Justin agreed to donate eleven of the pups to their program. The director got teary-eyed and thanked them for all they were doing to support the cause. They'd be placed with trainers at twelve weeks, to begin their instruction, but Carina was already starting to work with them.

Jason and Gia sold six pups to breeder/handlers for show dogs, kept two puppies, and then gave two to Carina. Justin decided to keep two pups for he and Charlotte to raise together. Three Great Danes might be a lot for either of their houses, but they were so attached they couldn't let them all go.

Justin watched Charlotte work in the kitchen with Gia and her friends for hours the night before Thanksgiving with a shit-eating grin on his face. She fit right in with the girls and told him repeatedly how nice it was to have girlfriends. He often wondered what her life was like before she'd moved here, but she was really evasive if he asked too many questions. He decided it was better he didn't know. He knew all he needed— that he was head over heels in love with her and ready to take the next step.

"Dude. I recognize that look," Jason said, intruding on his thoughts. He elbowed his twin in the gut.

"What? Watching." He wasn't ready for another lecture from Jason.

"All I was going to say is we love her too, man, and I know once Mom and Dad meet her tomorrow, they're going to love her just as much. Do we need to go ring shopping?"

Justin laughed, but damn if his twin hadn't honed right in on his thoughts. It was quick, sure. But if Justin had learned anything in his thirty years, it was that time didn't stand by and wait for you to make up your mind. It could all be over in a flash. Almost was for him. He didn't want to miss the opportunity to make Charlotte as happy as she'd made him.

"Shopping. Soon. Friday."

"Black Friday?! Are you fucking crazy? Why not just use Grandma's ring? I would have, but Gia and I eloped. There wasn't time for the whole engagement thing, we just did it."

Justin laughed. Their Grandma had passed away just after they'd graduated from high school. Before she died, she'd made sure to tell them that she wanted them to toss a coin to decide who got the ring for their girl. "No fighting," she'd said. "And you better not waste it on an unworthy girl. I'll know and I'll come back to haunt you if you do!"

Charlotte was completely worthy. She'd come to mean everything to him. He thought he just might need to make that phone call to Mom and ask her to bring it when they came tomorrow.

That night, he and Charlotte had a great time playing after she'd made pies with the girls. He grabbed a bottle of whipped cream from her fridge and chased her through the house, claiming he only wanted *her* pie. The whipped cream interfered with the way she tasted, though, and he couldn't have that.

When he'd finished bringing her to her second orgasm of the night, she turned the tables and used the whipped cream on him to tease him into a state of near-madness. She was quite talented with her tongue, he soon learned, and when he got close to losing it, she grabbed his hips so he couldn't back away, taking him all in until his legs gave out and he couldn't hold himself up any longer. They collapsed together on the bathroom floor on her furry mat and laughed until their bellies ached.

"Love. Charlotte."

"Love you," she replied, biting down on his chin.

"Love that," he moaned, but had no strength left to do more than kiss her gently.

They showered and fell into bed together, exhausted. That night, he dreamed about the accident, only this time when he lay in the water, he didn't feel as if he were going to drown. Instead, arms and legs wrapped around him from behind and long locks of hair swirled around his face. He turned his head to see it was Charlotte, and as her lips descended on his, he could breathe again. He tried to turn in her embrace to pull her close, but some force dragged her away into the darkness of the water below. He screamed for her, thrashing until his lungs felt as if they were being squeezed—

"Hey," Charlotte said, shaking him gently. "You were dreaming. Are you okay?"

"Pulled away. No. Charlotte stay."

He remembered her startled expression vividly, when he woke up the next morning. The dream had been on some kind of rewind the whole night, each time ending the same. He'd wakened with a horrid headache and agreed to let her use her magic fingers to massage his neck until he could function.

"Sorry. Woke you. Bad."

"I know. I could tell. You were screaming. Do you remember what it was about?"

He blinked. He couldn't tell her. He refused to try to get the words out, fearing he'd doom himself to the dream coming true. He couldn't lose her now, not after she'd completed his life. He knew he could go on without her, but he didn't want to.

Justin's parents arrived around two in the afternoon and they fawned all over Charlotte. They asked her a million questions so quickly she couldn't even get any answers out. Luckily, Gia saved the day by bringing them out back. Soon they were surrounded by fur balls and completely in puppy love. Justin mouthed "thanks" to Gia and she winked at him. This was one time he didn't mind her coming in for the save.

The six of them ate dinner and shared stories and laughter until they were all bursting at the seams. It was chilly outside, the Bay Area autumn finally choosing to set in on this night. They retired to the first-level patio around the fire pit, which they couldn't use yet as there were too many pups to watch. Jason turned on a standing gas heater instead, which provided ample warmth for the six of them. Gia turned on the lights that lined the yard and they all settled into the cushioned seats to cuddle and chat.

"Justin?" Gia said, remembering something. "I'm thinking we could use some of the extra blankets from up in your cottage for the pups tonight. The temperature is supposed to drop into the thirties possibly. I know they've got plenty of bodies to keep them warm. I was just thinking it would be a good idea."

"Yeah," Justin answered, taking his arm out from behind Charlotte as he stood.

"I'll help," Charlotte said, following him to the steps. Justin heard his mother murmur her approval to his dad. All night she'd been watching the two of them together with a satisfied smile on her face. She had told him the night before on the phone that she wouldn't give him the ring until she'd met the girl herself.

"I know you're a grown man," she'd laughed. "I just want the best for my boys." He'd groaned but agreed to go along with her wish. He didn't want to rush into anything... Okay, yes he did. But he could wait. A day or so. She had brought it with her, so maybe tomorrow...

Justin climbed the steps ahead of Charlotte, in a hurry to get back to the snuggling. They had to maneuver around pups who tried to follow them.

He was just scooting one to the side when he lost his footing.

***

Charlotte knew what was happening probably before Justin did.

When his foot slipped on the step and his weight pulled him backwards, all Charlotte could think was that a fall from this height would kill him for sure if he hit his already fragile head.

She reacted swiftly, putting herself in his path, catching his full one hundred eighty pounds.

Their bodies seemed to be pulled toward the ground in slow motion. Shrieks came from their right as Gia and his mom saw them falling.

The ground was unforgiving when Charlotte's back slammed into it. The air escaped from her and she felt the crack of her skull against the concrete. Everything went black...

Voices surrounded her. Angry voices. Yelling voices.

"You absolutely cannot take her from him like this," a heavily accented male voice shouted. "It is completely wrong and immoral. He's not strong enough, and by George, she deserves more than four weeks of happiness."

"You know the rules, Louis," a familiar grandmotherly voice said. "You and Maggie knew that this was a possibility. Neither of you can intervene—"

"This is bullshit, Grandma. Pardon my French. But he's right. I promised her—"

"Something you had no authority to do. Charlotte has made a sacrifice and she's prevented the death of one who is meant to go on and do greater things. That was the purpose of this intervention."

Charlotte tried desperately to open her eyes, but then fought the urge. She couldn't bear seeing the dingy gymnasium now, not after she'd found a love—

"But how can that be enough? What if this wrecks him? What if the guilt is too much and he can't go on? I'm sorry, but I saw how feeling as if you're the cause of someone's death, even if it's totally impossible that you were, can ruin a person. My brother would have died had he not found Jaylene. Star? He would have died had Louis and I—"

"Alright, alright. I see your point. I too wanted to see Charlotte find happiness. I had hoped for her to have a full life, rather than being cheated again as she was in her first. Let me see what I can do."

Charlotte faded in and out of consciousness. She heard Maggie and Louis arguing in hushed voices. She heard Justin's frantic pleas for help. The voices were warbled, like they would be under water, and her limbs felt as though they were floating. Any other time it would have been peaceful, like the time she went to Bucks Lake with her family when she was in middle school. She'd floated out in the middle of the lake for so long, her father had had to swim out to make sure she was okay.

"Sorry, Daddy," she'd said. *"It's just so peaceful out here."*

"You can't stay out here forever," he'd warned. *"You'll get too tired and not be able to swim back. Now come on, your mother's worried."*

She swam back with him, sad to leave her special place. Water had always given her peace, until she was too sick to swim. Then it was baths. She always preferred them to showers because the pounding of the spray hurt her sensitive skin.

She just needed to float for a while, and then she'd be as good as new…

Except this time, the longer she floated, the more pain she felt in her body and her head. It felt way different than it had when she'd been reborn.

Justin! She couldn't leave him now. Didn't ever want to leave him. She…

"Charlotte. Good. Eyes. Open." She felt pressure on her hand and it reminded her of the way Justin would squeeze a little too tightly sometimes, not able to control the pressure. She wished it was really his hand and that he could pull her out of the water.

"Breathe," she heard him say, and she tried to obey.

Suddenly something shifted and she gasped in a huge breath, her lungs starving for oxygen. She opened her mouth to speak but only managed to suck in more air.

"Please. Eyes. Charlotte. Love. Charlotte. Please."

I'm trying so hard. Don't let go.

It took a few more breaths before her eyes popped open and she glanced around wildly.

"Thank God. Stay. Don't go."

Justin's eyes were trained on her so intensely, it was as if he'd known just what had happened. He knew she'd almost been taken from him.

"Stay. Justin." She smiled faintly and then winced.

"Don't move," Justin's mom, Angela, said. "I'm a nurse. Let's make sure you didn't break anything."

Charlotte kept eye contact with Justin, who looked ready to tear his hair out with worry as his mother examined her for any broken bones. He refused to move away, staying next to Charlotte's side. She barely heard Angela say that she should go to the hospital, that she may have a concussion.

"We'll drive her," Jason said before running in the house.

Angela helped Charlotte sit up slowly. Her back ached a little, but she felt completely fine otherwise. She wasn't bleeding. She didn't feel weak. She got to her feet and walked around slowly, feeling no dizziness.

"I'm really okay," Charlotte said, smiling like a loon at Justin, who still held her hand.

"Go hospital. Get checked."

"I promise you, I'm really fine. I'm shocked, but I'm okay! Please. I just want to stay with you."

Justin pulled her in tightly, hugging her so close it could have been considered indecent in present company. He pulled back, only to bring his hands to her face and kiss her. And kiss her. And kiss her until she had to tap out for air.

"Love. Charlotte. Stay."

"I love you, Justin."

***

The moments it took for Charlotte to breathe again were the most frightening of Justin's life. Somehow he knew that she'd been given back to him. There was no way she should have walked away from that fall with no damage, especially when he'd landed on her with his full weight. He'd been on the top step, making it at least a five to six foot drop. And he'd heard her head crack on the ground. It was the most horrific sound he'd ever heard in his life.

He'd rolled off of her, completely unharmed, and thought for sure she'd been dead. When he couldn't find a pulse in her neck and he knew she wasn't breathing, he did something he hadn't done since he was a boy.

He prayed.

He hadn't even prayed for himself when he'd been hurt. He hadn't tried to bargain with God for his faculties to return. He accepted it as it was, felt there was a reason for everything. He even felt as if there was a reason Charlotte had come into his life when she did.

So he prayed that he could keep her. Selfish, sure. But he knew there was a reason she'd come and that they still had so much left to do and experience together. He felt stronger than ever with her by his side. That had to mean something.

He knew someone upstairs was listening when her eyes opened and she smiled at him.

Epilogue

Interview with Rivers singer Justin Rivers, and his twin brother, bassist Jason Rivers.
Feedback Magazine
Sammara Gunderson
Castro Valley, California
February 2015

Indie rock fans around the world have been holding their collective breath waiting for news from the band Rivers. After nearly losing his life in a terrible motorcycle accident in April of last year, Justin Rivers assures me it's a miracle he's able to talk to me today.

FM: Justin, I understand you are still experiencing speech issues from your accident, but that you can understand me clearly, is that correct?

Justin: Yes. Clear. Speech affected. Better now. Broca's Aphasia.

FM: Broca's Aphasia. That's a condition where speech is agrammatical and halted, but still mostly makes sense, correct?

Justin: Done. Research.

FM: I wanted to know how best to prepare for meeting you. Is there anything you want to tell your fans about your experience?

Justin: Difficult. Wanted give up. Kept trying. Speech therapy. Hours. Every day. Found love. Found hope. Better every day.

FM: I can tell by your smile that something very special is blossoming here.

Justin: Charlotte. Love…saved me.

FM: Then we all have her to thank! How does all of this affect the band? I understand you guys are back in the studio and nearly finished recording your next album.

Justin: Sing…fine. Play…not. Jason?

Jason: Justin can still sing; in fact, I'd even say his voice is stronger than ever. Broca's Aphasia occurs when there's been an injury to the left brain. Since music is primarily a right-brain function, he is in great shape. The only thing that has been majorly affected is his ability to play guitar. His hands don't have the same dexterity, so we talked about it and decided that we'd bring on a new guitar player, Ray, who we met through mutual friends. Simon, who has toured with us in the past, has agreed to take on the drum slot permanently, so we're back and more solid than ever.

FM: Right, because in the past, you two did all of the writing and recording alone, is that right?

Jason: We did. But adding two really tight musicians to the band full time has given our sound a boost. That wasn't something we'd counted on. We're pleasantly surprised.

FM: I understand there's been a whole lot of activity here for the past few months. Great Dane puppies? Readers can't see this, but they are everywhere!

Justin: Twenty-three. Crazy. Both girls pregnant. Same. Born night. Hands full!

FM: I bet! Wow! Twenty-three? What are you going to do with that many dogs?

Justin: Donated. Eleven. Service dogs. Training. Important. Blossom.

Jason: Blossom is Justin's dog. He had her before the accident, but she's really stepped up to take care of him. It gave him a purpose to get well. They're very close and she's helped him when his headaches occur. Yeah, we've donated eleven pups for training, gave away a few, and the rest are going to be show dogs. My wife Gia and I have been breeding and showing them for some time. We'll be slowing down soon, though. We're about to have our hands full again.

FM: Yes, I heard. Congratulations. Twins, right?

Jason: Yes, ma'am. Rivers runs deep in the gene pool.

Justin: Funny. Charlotte. Twins.

FM: You guys, too?

Justin: Yes. Married New Year's. Pregnant month later. Same Jason.

Jason: Yes indeed. Our parents have agreed to move back to help us out in the beginning. We'll likely put off heavy touring until after they're all born, maybe even beginning of 2016, but we *are* going to play some festivals this spring.

FM: Will we get to hear new material this spring?

Justin: Count on it.

FM: Excellent! Justin, I understand you'll be doing some different touring as well this year.

Justin: Yes. Speech. Talk vets. Traumatic Brain Injury. Sing for them. Encourage therapy.

FM: I think that's a wonderful way to make a difference. I've done some traveling with Jonathan Davis of Korn to see veterans still in the hospital. Many of them suffer from similar problems.

Justin: Kids. See kids. Therapy. Bring Blossom.

FM: You mean kids who have—

Jason: He's going to visit some groups for kids who have speech issues. Many children with Autism go through speech therapy because they are either nonverbal, or they speak but have trouble communicating or understanding social cues. Justin's therapist works with some local groups and thought he might be a great person to come and meet with the kids. Teach them songs, help them communicate when they can't find the words. It's something he still has trouble with sometimes, although he hasn't had a spell where he completely loses speech in a really long time. Not since Charlotte, right?

Justin: Charlotte. Good. Frustrating. Think clearly... can't... words. Find words. Make sense.

FM: It sounds like 2015 is going to be a busy year for you all. I can't wait to hear the new album and see you guys on the road. Thanks for taking time to chat with *Feedback* today.

Justin: Thank. Sammara.

Jason: Thank you very much. Stay tuned for more Rock 'n' Roll!

Thanks…and a final note on Blossomed

I was inspired to write this story to benefit Autism Awareness and it was originally going to be part of an anthology. The theme we were given was New Life. There are many aspects in the story that fit that theme, and it grew into quite a labor of love. I did research on folks with traumatic brain injury after a good friend experienced a similar accident as my hero, Justin. I watched videos of Gabrielle Gifford, a former U.S. Representative who was shot in Arizona in 2011, as she went through speech therapy, attempting to overcome aphasia. I admire the strength and courage she and others in her position have shown. My stepfather experienced aphasia for a brief time after having a stroke in his mid-30s, an event that profoundly affected our family. I began to think about being trapped in your own brain and how frustrating that would be. I write to express myself, I speak, I even sing. I also count myself as fortunate, and pray for those who struggle every day to do what comes naturally to me.

On the lighter side, while I was writing this story, a friend's Harlequin Great Dane had been bred and we were waiting to see if she was pregnant. The thought of having puppies around was so exciting. She became the model for my canine heroine and I enjoyed lots of cuddle time with her. I spoke to my vet, Dr. Jasmine Morris at VCA Lewelling Animal Hospital, and to my mother-in-law, Lynda, about the experience of whelping pups and I am grateful to them for sharing their wisdom. I learned that Great Danes are indeed known for large litters. In one story I read, a woman's dam had seventeen!

My mother-in-law has taught me so much about dogs from her experiences showing and breeding them for many years. When I met her, she had the most amazing English bulldog named Blossom. She bred her shortly before I met her, and my husband and I were lucky enough to raise two of her pups, Zeus and Celie. I miss them both very much. Blossom was one of my favorite dogs ever, so I decided to memorialize her in this story. I hope you enjoy reading it as much as I did writing it.

Blossom
April 1992–January 2005

Read the story that started this whole new world... Rereleasing May 13, 2016 with bonus material. Meet Maggie and Louis and catch up with the gang from Haunted.

Minded

to look after; take care of; tend
to mind one's kin

November 2013

"My name is Maggie and I'm a ghost. I guess. Damn, I sound like I'm at a twelve-step program."

"You are, my dear. A support group, really. Please continue."

Maggie looked around at the circle of folks in the dingy gymnasium and wished for a scalding-hot shower. The room was so dark outside of their circle of creaky metal chairs that she couldn't see whether they were surrounded by bleachers, windows, doors... Nothing. The scuffed wood floor with markings for basketball was the only indicator of what type of room this was. She wondered if she were to throw a coin out into the darkness, would it hit anything?

The others in the circle were dressed in a variety of ways, indicating what they had been doing before they ended up in the circle, Maggie supposed. Suits, coveralls, yoga pants. Eek. To be stuck in yoga pants for an eternity. Fashion faux pas to the max!

"What do you want me to say?" she exclaimed, irritated to the point of wanting to scratch her skin off. Some of the others fidgeted in their seats. They moved as though their asses were numb from sitting too long.

"Whatever comes to mind. You have been sent here because of your D.D.S." The plump, grandmotherly woman in the pale-pink turtleneck sporting a steel-gray bun was quickly becoming the focus of Maggie's irritation.

"My orthodontist? Why the hell is he still after me? We paid him!"

"Death Denial Syndrome. It happens quite frequently, you know. Especially to stuck-up party girls such as yourself," a grumpy, heavily accented male voice said from behind a mop of black hair. He was sitting two spots over from Maggie so she hadn't quite noticed him until he spoke. She had no idea where she was. How did she end up here? Maggie was very confused.

"You lot come in here 'like, whatever! Gag me with a spoon!'"

Maggie attempted to turn in her chair, but only succeeded in swiveling her torso to face him. "Okay, Mr. Nineteen Eighties! I know I died. I'm not a complete moron." Whoever this guy was, he was oozing attitude from every pore of his denim-clad body. His bangs fell in his eyes, hiding half of his face, so Maggie couldn't tell if he had anything to back up all that attitude. But The Dead Kennedys, Minor Threat, and Fear patches, along with several other patches and buttons from late-'70s/early-'80s punk bands sewn onto the ratty denim vest, gave a little bit of a clue.

"Margaret, dear, what Louis is trying to say—"

"It's Bones," Mr. 1980s interrupted.

"Shut up! Your name is not Bones," Maggie said with a laugh and a flip of the hair. "That's so funny! I manage a band—"

"Managed. Emphasis on the 'ed'. You're dead, lady. You don't do shit anymore. That's why you're here."

Maggie frowned and crossed her ankles, the slight move all she could manage to complete. Her Louboutins were cutting into the back of her heels, as they had done forever, and her black party dress was constricting. It had been a long night, even before she'd ended up here. She wished she were naked in her own bed, cuddled up next to—

"So I'm dead. Fine. Whatever. Why am I here?"

Grandma smiled kindly and laced her fingers in her lap. "You are here, Margaret, because in order to exit from this existence, you must be prepared to purge your earthly ties and accept the choice you must make."

"Choice? Fine. I choose to leave here and get back to work. My boys need me."

Louis sighed, exasperated. "Lady, you need to get a clue. You're gone. Your 'boys' have moved on, and that's that."

Maggie pushed her blonde curls out of her face. "If you know so much, why are *you* here?"

Louis sat up from his slouch and ran his fingers through the black mop hanging in his eyes. Maggie gasped. Underneath that black hair was the face of an angel. Okay, not a real angel. More like a punk-rock, rebel-without-a-cause, bad-boy fallen angel. The complete opposite of her husband. *Thomas.*

"Where's Thomas? Where's my husband?" She tried to stand up, but felt as though she were weighted down. "Why can't I go? What is this place?"

"A holding cell? Purgatory? Whatever your theology calls it. It's a shite hole we can't leave until we've 'moved on'."

"Thank you, Louis. Margaret, your death was tragic, and just as your life touched so many people, your death affected them profoundly as well. They are struggling without you."

"Then let me out of here so I can go back to work! God! What is wrong…why can't I move?" She was never prone to hysterics, but she was fixin' to beg like a dog at the table if it meant she could see her boys again.

"The power to move is all in your hands. You must accept the way things are and embrace your destiny."

Maggie was always up for a challenge. She didn't make it to the top of her game in the music industry by sitting back and taking it in the ass. She wasn't about to sit back and take it now.

Connect with R.L. Merrill

I would love to connect with you! Here's where you can find me lurking: Facebook at:
www.facebook.com/rowritesrocknromance
Email at rlmerrillauthor@gmail.com
Twitter @rlmerrillauthor
And my groovy website: www.rlmerrillauthor.com where you can find my newsletter-y thingie and stay up-to-date with the latest from my world of Rock 'n' Romance! You can even pick up passwords to unlock short stories set in the Teacher, Haunted and The Rock Season worlds.

Reviews

Reviews are incredibly important to authors. If you enjoyed Blossomed: A Minded Story please leave your review for others at Amazon, Goodreads, or whichever rooftop you'd like to shout it from!